WAITING FOR
FOR
TED

dead ink

First published in Great Britain in 2022 by Dead Ink,
an imprint of Cinder House Publishing Limited.

Print ISBN 9781915368003
Ebook ISBN 9781915368010

Editing by Ella Chappell
Proofreading by Dan Coxon
Cover design by Luke Bird
Typeset by Laura Jones

Printed and bound in Great Britain by Clays Ltd, Elcograf S.p.A.

www.deadinkbooks.com

WAITING FOR TED

MARIEKE BIGG

dead ink

PROLOGUE

Soft, bright, ethereal, I stand in the glow of a hot stove. Sun blasts through a panelled window, the shadow of bars projected on the floor in front of me, connoting church or prison, the light bathing me in angelic charm. I am tall. I am magnificent; a voluptuous centrepiece amidst the dazzle of scintillating dust lifting me to the heavens. I am housewife. My pink, frilly apron bounces with fertility, its tie accentuating my waist, reminding you that these curves could bear your children. My hair is thick, locks cascading down my shoulders like a fountain of youth, framing a wide-eyed face that is at your service. I am superwife. The kind who labours preparing sweaty meat for hours, and comes out with her pastels still pristine, her skin still smelling of Chanel. Innocence and servitude in a frilly wrapper. So sweet you'd give her to a child to eat. Only when you look a little closer, you notice a hint of lace exposed by a small gape of her apron, the trimming of a fishnet stocking against seductively smooth leg. You look again and suddenly the food she is preparing is all suggestively phallic. Sausages pulsating in their casserole dish; short, fat root vegetables squirming from the cutting board; bananas bending in the fruit-bowl on the side. You suddenly notice her plump pink lips, primed for the blowjob she'll give you after dinner. This is the Stepford Wife. Her interiors lighting up your Instagram with ironic dreams of domestic charm – the baking, the home, and a little extra; pink frills meet leather and fur. The detail is in defiance. Domestic frivolity for the twenty-first century.

The Stepford Wife is alluring but, also, slightly unhinged. Sometimes, when you look at her too long, you worry that she'll leap out from the picture on your phone. As if she could crack through the shiny screen with her leather flogger and grab you with her long nails. But you're safe really. That's part of her appeal. She remains perfectly still in her perfection, already waiting for you to look at her, to double tap her with your thumb or index finger, whichever it is you use to tell her that you like her. She remains there in her unassuming antici- pation, just on the off chance that, perhaps, you'll peruse a few more of her photographs. Maybe you'll rein her in even tighter, decide to follow her account, so that she is fixed even firmer in the grip of your approval, and you continue to watch her there, everything she does, all of her. As long as you both shall live.

ONE

There are plenty of accounts to gawk over, but my favourite, my absolute guru, is Mrs.Ladyfriend. I want her life. She doesn't have the biggest following out there, but her interiors are so warm, her photos perfect compositions of fruit and foliage and furniture, all taken from her beachside home in Malibu. And her husband is always absent from the frame. Her account is about her and the life she is creating, how she is cultivating that identity not through her husband, but alongside him. She is #empowered. And she is reaching out to other women who want to do the same. She is there first and foremost for other women. I *felt* that when I first came across her account; I *got* her. I saw a photo of striped, nautical teacups against a pastel-themed kitchen and a view over the Pacific Ocean and I was sold. Expand your horizons. The sky's the limit.

I look around my living room from my spot on the chaise longue. My showroom in its latest guise. I'd discovered Instagram not long after I discovered furniture outlets. "Terribly suburban," Mum would have said, by which she meant that the stuff you buy from those places was too "vulgar", by which she meant, too cheap to impress her friends. But the idea that you could visit a place that offered you visions of countless potential lives appealed to me. Discovering that there was a virtual equivalent just a tap and a scroll away was nothing short of a revelation. Ten years later, I'm not just drawing inspiration, but providing it, to a following that could rival that of any celebrity interior designer. Admittedly, my relationship with Ted may not be everything I hoped for, but of my Instagram, I am very proud.

Always perfectly on-trend, my living room usually evokes the kind of existential peace that comes with knowing that you are exactly where you ought to be. This morning, though, as I look around the space between four walls that had so long been a perfect projection of the image of my eye, it is now a sombre, shadowy pit. It isn't just the colour, which is all wrong – icy blue, crystal and grey – it's also the architecture of the space: the windows, usually inspiring reverence, the way they reach for the sky, look suddenly poky and small; the room so narrow and the ceilings so low. I wonder suddenly how I'd ever managed to walk through it upright. I rub the back of my neck.

I have to admit it to myself. Things don't feel right. Not in here; not between me and Ted. Interiors are deeply symbolic. They tell you all you need to know. Mine is sending me chilling threats, warning me to take my relationship into my own hands, to rise to the challenge. A bath is a good idea.

Tina had told me to take a bath. Tina, our next-door neighbour, is twenty years my senior at least, although I'm not sure exactly – she's never mentioned her age. Her face is disorientating, a prism of times and places, of colour and light. She is always ornamented. A quixotic collection on legs, a walking museum of empresses' jewels and pharaohs' bangles – so clad in distractions that I can never remember what she looks like. Only the emeralds of her eyes stick; they lurk in my subconscious with penetrating clarity.

"Understand that men will treat you differently now," Tina had told me. Tina is real. Not like the childhood backstabbers who just told you what you wanted to hear, then gossiped about you behind your back. "You're going to need a different strategy." Tina is wise, a veteran of a bygone era of incontrovertible truths. Forty years of marriage later, her husband is now dead, which gives her total authority on the facts of her relationship. That suits her well.

"The thing is… undying affection, it's an unfortunate phrase." She cast her eyes to the ground, evoking her own tragic loss. "Romance is a mortal condition. It comes and goes with our aching, withering bodies, and so if we want it to survive, we have to be realistic. Strategic, even. You've passed your peak, Rosalind. Ted is going to need further incentive. You're going to have to put more skin in the game."

I squirmed. "Skin?"

She nodded. Serene. Distinguished. "Skin, darling, is a canvas. You must use it."

Tina knew me well by now. Knew which metaphors to use. It had occurred to me recently that, if I'd done what my parents had wanted and continued my education instead of moving in with Ted, I would have studied art. Pictures, paintings and sculptures make a great deal of sense to me. It is something about the undeniable pleasure they evoke. Incontrovertible. Art has to be static. Film doesn't have the same effect on me – too slippery, fleeting. There is no assurance in that.

I didn't end up studying art. And with good reason. Love and art had never been diametrically opposed. Ted is a means to the same end. There is something very aesthetic about a relationship.

Ted fits into the picture I am trying to paint. I like how he looks in a button-up shirt. "Terribly suburban," Dad would always say about his appearance, by which he meant that it was "vulgar", by which he meant that Ted didn't earn enough to be deemed acceptable, tie or no tie. But I don't care that Ted is just an estate agent and not the owner of an estate. This isn't the 1800s – to my parents' great dismay. Their substantial inheritance had allowed them to exist in a time vacuum, an era of landed gentry, of dark, dusty drawing rooms full of fading trinkets, of dull china and gloomy pheasant for dinner. For the rest of humanity, however, that time had passed. To be replaced by a new kind of glamour. The glamour of a photo that anyone can take; the internet is a universally accessible canvas. Something that connects us all. Like skin.

Ted's job doesn't matter – that, I am still convinced of. But I have by now accepted the less romantic reality: that it is going to take more than a pretty picture to make life together bearable. That I need more than his presence in a photograph to make this work.

I looked at Tina who looked at me. She was taking me in. Scrutinising. I shifted in my seat, there, in my neighbour's front room. Compelled, suddenly, to explain myself. I searched for the right words but found myself stating the banal facts of the situation that mattered to me least – "He's just gone a lot."

She nodded as she sipped coffee from a china cup. Her interior was what some might call eclectic, others gaudy: gold-rimmed mirrors and cast-bronze lions beside mock-Roman pillars framing an already-blazing fireplace. She hadn't updated it since her husband had died, I was sure of it; which made me wonder in my more suspicious moments if she was as stoic as she let on. Still mourning her loss, perhaps. A mere mortal despite the dazzling façade. An interior is deeply symbolic.

"Where does he go?" she asked, distinctly uninterested, as though she already knew.

I looked away.

"Don't worry. Relationships are like sculpting. You chisel away at them year after year and end up with an amateurish attempt at perfection." She looked over at the urn on the fireplace with what I thought for a second might be remorse. The urn was the only aspect of the room I'd ever liked. It was ancient, with snake-like dragons carved into bronze-coloured stone. Manchurian, perhaps. I wasn't sure. Whatever it was, it was an odd choice for her husband's resting place. Somehow effeminate, like she'd chosen it for herself, not him. Not that it really mattered to him now, of course. We both let our eyes settle on the thing for a while, until a flash of movement, a shadow of a bird or a ghost fluttering by, and the ticking of the clock snapped me back.

"Work," she said, wagging her finger at me. "It takes work." She put her cup down on the mahogany side table and leaned in from her gilded throne. She peered at me over her narrow glasses, her eyes moving up and down me like a metal detector. "As I suspected."

I put my hand to my cheek, searching for the source of her prognosis.

"What is it?"

"A chin hair."

I looked at her. "So?"

"Personal grooming is illustrative. You've got the wrong attitude."

I liked it when she scolded me. For a second her certainty was my own. I observed Tina. She practised what she preached. Even when I dropped in on her on early mornings with mis-delivered packages, she was the picture of polish, makeup intact, perfume to match. Her skin was smooth, coated in a thin layer of powder, just enough for a subtle finish, stopping short of clown-like, the way so many women looked today. She herself was a misplaced relic from the past, too glamorous for this unimaginative suburb, so much so that I often wondered how she had ended up here. You could never dare to ask her about her origins, of course; that would be offensive, would somehow imply that you doubted the authenticity of her place-less, ageless wisdom.

"Here's my advice, darling. Go home, bathe, lather yourself in whatever lotions and potions you can find. Fill in the cracks. Smoothen out the crevices."

"Crevices!" I cried. But Tina didn't entertain girlish panic. I was much too old for that.

"Make yourself look the way you did when he first met you." Her shrewd glare stripped me bare, scouring my body for all its fleshy faults.

I looked back at her, now very conscious of the bags under my eyes. I let the moment linger. She was an intuitive woman; I was sure she'd catch the question that still hovered between us. *What if it was too late?*

She returned my gaze with a steady sea-green tranquillity.

"Go home," she said.

I put my coffee cup down and stood up, buzzed from an infusion of caffeine and sheer panic; a blend I was sure Tina didn't understand was the driving force of my generation. I scurried to the front door. She stopped me just as I was about to walk out.

"And Rosalind–"

I stopped and turned.

"I think it would be advisable that you don't return here until you have managed to procure a ring for that finger. It will be crucial, in fact, for me to believe that you are taking this all seriously."

I looked down at my naked hand, like I'd already failed. I shuffled out of the door. I walked on down the narrow path, up to the white picket fence, out onto the pavement, five steps more and I turned to face the almost identical house that was my own.

I stopped. It was not exactly the same. I'd made quite a few improvements. It was still, even after all these years, quite perfect. The quaint image of domestic simplicity I'd always wanted. It got a fresh coat of paint every year, I made sure of it, with glossy woodwork – blue and pink. I'd wanted it to look like one of the houses in *The Stepford Wives*. Further evidence that I'd created my own nightmare. There was something about the terror of frilly hyper-femininity that made me feel in control. Something about the image of myself in the dewy light of a brisk autumn morning baking a pie that made the repression and rage I knew I'd feel in doing it fictional, manageable; desirable, even.

Don't choose the qualities you want in a man; they only last as long as he makes an effort (a timespan you can reliably estimate based on his longevity in the sack). Choose the flaws you want to put up with. Perfection only exists on the Gram. I'd chosen my perfectly imperfect life. Sensible. Pragmatic. So why had it gone so wrong?

TWO

I blink as I take in my living room a few moments more. Confronted with the sterile mess I've made, I have to be honest: Ted is losing interest in me. Tina is right. Things that he used to say were cute are now a source of acute irritation to him. He used to, if not support, at least humour my proclivity to artistic reinvention. He'd joke that our living room had changed its attire more often than a "woman in heat", then stroke my head and pat my bum and carry on whatever boyish activity he'd set himself to – video-gaming, beer-drinking, football-watching, Dorito-munching. Now, he seethes at every new piece of furniture that enters his house, even the rare finds, tells me I will ruin us, tells me it is all my fault.

It isn't like we are married or anything. No children. Besides sharing a house, there is nothing much preventing us from making a fairly clean cut if we want to. Only that doesn't feel like an option. There is something strangely final about the life we've built. What I assume people mean when they talk about "destiny".

I can see the toll it is taking on me. All I have to do is look in the mirror, the crow's feet spreading across my temples like talons determined to engulf my head. It is a threat of sorts, although, until today, it has been unclear what exactly they are threatening.

Ted is far from perfect. But there is competition to contend with. I'd seen the way women still look at him. His beer belly bulges almost triumphantly – nothing can break his masculine form. Despite his junk-food fuelled, inactive lifestyle, he has retained his broad shoulders, his arms hanging bow-shaped by his sides to make room for his still-noticeable biceps, and an expression always of slight befuddlement, which on a woman would look silly but on him is only endearing. It is also exactly the kind of semi-lucidity a woman can prey on. And I know that the bigger his gut gets, the smaller his ego, the more likely he is to accept their advances – seeking their validation although he barely knows it, oh-so-cluelessly.

It is my own doing, Tina would say. I've taken my eye candy and turned him into dough. I've given him nothing to fight for, a female counterpart so saggy nobody would bother to intercept.

Funny that I haven't noticed. Somehow, despite my fixation on my Instagrams, my own body has disappeared from the equation. My former school friends are in much better shape. It is easy to keep tabs. Over the years I'd witnessed an exodus of pristine, petite bodies onto social media. Not having to contend with anything as mundane as earning a living, these trust-fund babes were delighted to discover that showcasing your non-productivity had become a veritable profession in the digital age. One by one, the friends I thought I'd managed to shed had begun to populate my feeds, my stories, niggling at me with their workout videos; juicy bums levitating ever-higher, lips miraculously plumper with every snap. It is facile, not for me. I had opted instead for the seductive curve of a chair-leg, the gloss of a fine leather, the hump of an excellent pouf. "Love yourself," Jenny always tells me. Jenny: former best friend who'd become an influencer before I even knew how to post a story. She isn't beautiful in real life, at least I've never thought so. People don't like her either. She'd been the outcast hippy at a severely preppy private school, into yoga when it was still a filthy habit, before it had become a "lifestyle".

People find her more palatable as a picture. Without her whiny voice piercing the air with nonsense about "chakras", her audience were suddenly open to her feel-good version of life. "Love yourself," she'd DM me, and I'd show myself considerable self-gratitude for not meeting up with her in person. I know how that would be. She'd take one look at my frazzled appearance and tell me I'd let myself go. She wasn't allowed to say that. Tina could, because she knows what she is talking about, because she has my best interests at heart. Jenny doesn't really care about anyone, wouldn't tolerate actually listening to my problems, or as she calls it, "negativity".

Tina knows that problems are part of life, part of love, part of making a relationship work. Now I understand that too. After all these years, I am surprised to find that we are still in that process of trying to assemble two fully self-sustaining parts into one. It had been an overall daunting task, only compounded by the merging of assets when we'd decided to move in together. I still remember that day all those years ago when, faced with the stack of cardboard boxes marked "Ted", or "Rosie", I'd felt a sudden swelling pressure to make the right decisions about what to keep and what to throw away. An inordinate burden weighed on me to make sure we salvaged the best of both. An ominous premonition, a wisp and a slither passing through me, that if I got it wrong, there would be hell to pay.

THREE

I'm waiting for Ted to come home. He is at work, on a Saturday, which seems suspicious, but I've learnt to give him the benefit of the doubt; not because I'd been proven right in the past but because it was the only way I'd stay sane. Besides, his being away gives me time to prepare.

As much as I trust Tina's intentions, her suggestion that a quick makeover would fix years of pent-up resentment is surely oversimplifying the matter. Maybe I am just afraid, though – that it wouldn't work, that I've let it go too far. That I am irrevocably rotten. I shake myself out of it. Never mind all of that now. A bath never hurts. People were better when they were relaxed, even made better decisions. Jenny had said that, probably in a random post or in some context that would have rendered it meaningless, but it makes sense to me now.

I hold my breath and set out to cross the living room, focusing my attention on the stairs ahead, clenching my teeth to fight the cold. Once on the other side, I dart up the stairs, heading for the bathroom, almost tripping on the final step, and stumble onto the landing, steadying myself on the cold white wall until, finally, I reach the bathroom, shut the door behind me, and turn on the hot tap. I sigh. The water trickles before it pours, heating up as it does. I watch the brass tap fog up – still a good choice. Classic. It will never go out of style. If only I could say the same about my own appearance.

I add a few drops of essential oil to the running water so that the billowing clouds carry sweet lavender to my nose. The steam rouses me, wrenches me out of my pathetic state of self-pity. What had I been cowering for? What was I afraid of? Submission had never been my style. Not in bed; not in life. Aren't I the woman who, against the wishes of her parents, had left an existence of comfortable luxury and had chosen instead to live? Aren't I the bulldozer who, despite the disapproving scowls of her peers, had chosen a man and a life that were both courageously real? This is what it means to fight for survival. I stand panting in the thickening smog like a sumo wrestler gearing up for a fight, letting the vapour mix with sweat until my skin gleams as if coated in oil. I stand there, body tense in fighting stance, until the heat starts to make me dizzy. Only then do I turn off the tap and leave for the bedroom.

I am ready. It is time to take my clothes off. I pull my trousers down in one swift motion and wrestle my jumper over my head, then face the long mirror and drag my eyes down.

Jesus.

Is this really what a forty-year-old body looks like? I don't remember Mum's ever looking like this. I would have been twenty when she was forty. Old enough to understand at least the concept of fleeting youth. Sufficiently seething with loathing for my mother to have noticed anything sub-par. But as far as I can remember, at forty, she'd still been trim, skin still taut. And she always "made the best of it", always dressed in a two-piece or light cashmere on the weekends. Hair still thick and pinned into some configuration of an up-do most days. I'd always thought she'd lacked individuality, real style, but she'd kept herself looking respectable. I would have scoffed at such a word when I was younger, but it made sense to me now.

It makes sense because what I am facing here, in the stark light of a suburban Saturday, is anything but respectable. It is so ugly I am almost afraid to touch it. It isn't the image I'd left here ten years ago, the last time I'd properly looked in the mirror. It isn't just the saggy, deflated shape of it that I barely recognise – lumps in all the wrong places on a frail, hunched-over carcass – it is the colour, too. Faded, grey, like my soul has already fled. How hadn't I noticed?

Perhaps it is the discovery of wide-legged culottes that is to blame. Ted called them my "tent trousers" and had complained, when I first got them, about how the loose fabric hid my "pretty decent" bum. I had to admit that flattery had not been on my mind when I'd bought them. I'd seen them advertised, of course – slim, middle-aged women claiming they hid the bumps and accentuated the waist – but to me it was simply a revelation that trousers could be so loose-fitting, letting me bend over and shift furniture and paint walls without worrying about exposing myself in the process. Ted was right; they were a bit like a tent in that they let my legs roam free in their own little cosmos as I created mine. By now, Ted had stopped complaining about them. Maybe he'd realised what lay underneath.

Perhaps the culottes resembled a low point, but it had always been a point of pride to me that I don't show off my body the way other women did. Ted had said how that made me even more regal in the beginning. It is sexy, he says, getting just a glimpse and a peek; sexiness is all about what you couldn't see. Perhaps that is the problem. If sex appeal lies with mystery, then I'd obliterated every chance of passion between us. Ted lives inside of me; that is, our life together lays me bare for all, including him, to see. The house *is* me. Every cushion, every candle something I have chosen; every shade of paint a choice that bears my mood. Even the crinkles in the cushions, the folds in the blankets, the creases in the sheets can be read into my ageing skin. With Ted being so immersed in my insides all day, it is difficult to get him to see only my fishnet-fabric façade. I have no mystery left.

I can take comfort in the fact that, as much as I've become an emotional exhibitionist, my body remains my own. I hadn't sacrificed it to the male gaze, not me; I could in all honesty say that I've retained that degree of dignity. No matter how far Ted drifted, I have never coaxed him back with sex. I have stayed true to my own desires, refusing to sacrifice my body on the altar of male approval. I wonder if that is what Tina is really asking of me now: whether, for all her talk of pampering myself, she is really telling me to offer my body as living bait.

FOUR

I'm waiting for Ted to come home, shedding my old skin so that our relationship can do the same. Humans have transcended the animal world, after all. We don't have to rely solely on our own bodies' capacity for change. We have devices like pumice stone and epilators that can help reignite the fire within.

Sex with Ted had been good at first. He had this unnerving ability to arouse me. Like a puppeteer, he'd pull an imaginary string and my leg would just fly up in the air, another and my hip swung to the right, another and I came. It was like I was an extension of him. He animated me.

Sex with Ted was different from anything I'd known. He wasn't polite like the others. The boys from home had always peppered the experience with pleases and thank yous. Because that was what you did. Not because they cared. It made the whole thing oddly transactional. And for them it probably was. In that world it was all about who you knew and who you were seen with and who you were shagging. Private parts didn't exist. With Ted, human politics don't matter. We are carnal. He ravages me. Unapologetically. He especially likes doing it from behind, pounding me until I feel floppy and sloppy like a piece of meat. In those moments I imagine my vulva as two bits of pulsating bacon, and suddenly I know the meaning of true decadence.

I think he liked it too. I'd never been beautiful, slightly too pale and a face all disproportioned; a problem at school in the days before Instagram allowed you to compensate by "learning your angles", as Jenny always lectured. The boys had never been impressed by me, but Ted always said I had the appeal of a "Pre-Raphaelite princess". It surprised me that he even knew about the Pre-Raphaelites, but I assumed he'd seen some niche porn somewhere. It didn't matter, though. He thought I was a princess.

Royalty. That's what he thought we were. I explained to him the difference between landed gentry and aristocracy, a distinction going back to feudalism in the sixteenth century to distinguish between landowners and those with titles imbuing peerage, but it didn't seem to make a difference to him. "It doesn't matter," he'd say, scooping me into his sizeable arms. "You're my queen."

Having him over in the beginning had been awkward. There was always the compulsory dinner with guests carefully curated by my parents to fuel the next round of gossip surrounding their daughter's – temporary, they'd stress – rebellion.

Mum would scowl at Ted as he picked up the big fork for his starter. Dad would make a point of clarifying his education at each meal, asking Ted to "remind" him if it was "Oxford or Cambridge" he'd gone to "read… What was it again?" So that Ted would have to tell everyone there that estate agents didn't need degrees, that even if they did, he wasn't "bright enough for the top unis". A sentence that made even me squirm. Then Dad would say that it was most peculiar that anyone in the business of property would not read Land Economy at Cambridge, seeing that there was such a wealth – he made sure to use that word – of knowledge about the proper management of assets going all the way back to William the Conqueror. Then Ted would say that he didn't know anything about that. Then nobody would speak until the catering staff brought out the pheasant.

Nonetheless, things developed quickly between us. It was easier when we did things on his turf. He liked himself better and so I liked him better too. I made him take me places he liked. Told him it would be romantic, like in *Titanic* when Leo shows Kate what real living is. The modern-day knight in shining armour is a boy with street smarts, I told him, someone who could protect me if all the money and privilege was stripped away, if we were out at sea and it was just us against the beating waves.

"It won't be as exciting as all that," he'd tell me. He was right, of course. He hadn't risked life and limb exactly, but he had faced my dad, which was close to the same thing. And just his daily life was thrilling to me. He took me to the pub with his "mates". Not as a novelty but as *the* social happening of the week. His friends would bring their "missus", their "other halves", who were all wearing leopard print and leather and so much foundation they all sort of looked the same, and we'd sit there, drinking prosecco till our heads ached, laughing and showing off, and our "fellas" would just sit there, placid; no games or subterfuge, not like at home or at school, they just sat there, arms wrapped tightly around us. There was of course the occasional laddish "banter", their word for jokes at our expense, about how clueless we were, or how much we "nagged", but mostly they were just happy to be sitting there – relaxed, pleasantly sedated, by our sides.

I was nervous, the first time he brought me with him. It took me all of five minutes to commit my first faux pas, when instead of simply ordering "a pint", I asked to see the menu and chose a bottled IPA. To his friends I became the "posh bird" forevermore. I was just happy not to be excluded from their banter; it made me one of them. It was that easy. No codes or rules about cutlery or prerequisite degrees. And so, we spent more time with his friends than mine, and then eventually with his family too. I didn't like mine anyway.

Looking back now, I wonder if he liked me less out of my natural habitat, just as I had him. Perhaps the big house and the nasty parents had been a novelty to him as much as pubs were to me. Perhaps he liked me as a princess, not the girl next door.

I turn away from the mirror, taking a few deep breaths to alleviate the rising tension spreading from my chest and through my entire body. This is the "before", I tell myself. In the twenty-first century, birthrights don't matter. Royalty is a state of mind. I am about to transcend my material limitations, to transform myself into the princess Ted had once loved, but better. I am going to find my "goddess within". Jenny will love that. This will be a ritual of religious proportions. This time, Ted will not only be in awe; he'll be reverent. I walk naked into the dense bathroom air and dip a toe in the cauldron.

FIVE

I'm waiting for Ted to come home. Repenting for my sin of negligence; trying to become a better woman. I've discovered a new meaning to the phrase "baptism by fire". The water is scorching. I let my toe shrivel in the heat. I watch it go red like a pig-in-a-blanket before sinking in the rest of my foot, leg, torso, until I lie flat in the tub. I let the redness spread over my skin, imagine the view from above as my entire body turns raw besides the pasty circles around my nipples and my face still floating above the water. I hang here in suspension, wondering if my soul could be as ugly as I must look in this moment.

I know that no singular event ever breaks a couple. That Tina would say it was always a process. I'd noticed early on that my Ted wasn't going to satisfy the role I'd cast him in. He wasn't the man of action I'd imagined. It wasn't that he totally failed to deliver, but he always managed to underwhelm. He promised me a house, a picture-perfect dream of a house that we would make our own. For a while, my nights were filled with ecstatic visions of him sanding down the woodwork, of him digging up the garden shirtless, the hard labour transforming his sloppy gut into a glistening sixpack. In the end, we split the mortgage and I did the decorating while Ted was at work. That daily separation could have saved our romance had it sparked the lustful longing of lovers parted. After a day at the office, however, Ted chose Netflix over passion. Preferably with a bowl of instant noodles on his lap.

"I love a good noodle," he'd slobber, saucy slithers flopping against his chin, taunting me with their phallic cylindricality.

None of that, though, was decisive; they were all just blemishes on a still-salvageable canvas, barely even a scuff compared to that one pivotal evening. If I had to pick a moment that marked the beginning of our real, irreversible decline, it would have to be the night of the chicken.

It was a Friday night about a year or so after we'd merged our possessions. I'd cooked him dinner and was wearing lingerie for the first time in a while. I was in a good mood because I'd hit a landmark: 20,000 followers. The same as Jenny. The £200,567 investment in furniture and wallpaper and textiles and paint had paid off – I'd always told Ted it would. He'd never exactly challenged me, although I had noticed how he'd downed an extra three beers the night I accidently divulged the exact sum after I myself had inhaled a slightly too hefty glass of red. It was necessary – variation on a theme is key when building a brand, I'd told him. Shortly after that I learned of the game-changing possibility of buying followers. That really got the ball rolling, people just had to be pointed in the right direction in the first place. My empire was steadily building. Soon, brands would be paying me to redo my living room. That was the dream, I'd tell Ted most nights at dinner.

People liked the life I showed them. The Stepford Wife, that's how they knew me. And my brand really did say it all, who I was – housewifery was my rebellion. People finally appreciated that.

WAITING FOR TED

That night, the night of the chicken, I'd decided to hail in my era as a legitimate influencer in style, since style was now my area of professional expertise. I'd prepared a bird so plump it was almost sexual. I'd cooked it to perfection: glossy, with just the right amount of crunch. I started the process early, removing the chicken with time to spare. I observed it in its tray, surrounded by citrus fruits and sprigs of herbs and knew I had to take a picture. It just looked so idyllic: the warm brown flesh against hues of orange, yellow and green; tray resting on the stove, and a cactus on the windowsill behind it – the sexy, dangerous edge that made my account so distinctive. I posted it with the caption: "I have been loving preparing dinners for my hardworking hubby <3 What does your spouse like for dinner?", and then I added the hashtags:

#sexywife #femininity #femininewomen #homemaker #feminine #housewifelife #housewifey #femininesisters #femininefamily #femininity #femininefashion #femininewomen #femininewisdom #housewifelife #naturalfemininity#traditionalfemininity #femininityispower #femininewomanhood #sex

I was really getting the hang of hashtags. It had taken me a while to get to grips with their poetry, how they represented a balance between message and reach. Hashtags, I now understood, were the art of power. By quoting them you became part of a series of posts that gave them their meaning. Now, when people searched #homemaker, they'd eventually come across my chicken. That was real, formative participation. That was true influence.

The photo didn't need much editing; the yellow interior light brought out the spring-chicken palette very well. It all went so smoothly that after posting it I still found time to put on lipstick and spritz on some Chanel before sitting down at the table for 7:05, which was when Ted reliably got home in those early days. Then we'd always tell each other about our days, finding all the mutual understanding we needed, reassuring us every evening at dinner that we'd found a safe haven in a world fractured by class and idiocy, a world populated with people who were caught up in all the wrong things, who didn't understand the simplicity of a home and a chicken and two people bound simply by love.

Ted walked in perfectly on schedule and gave me the reaction I'd hoped for. Stuttering at the sight of my lace-trimmed legs, ravenous for the juicy meat I presented to him. It was only after two servings that I told him the good news.

"You're probably wondering what the occasion is," I said, eyelashes fluttering.

He licked the gravy from the corner of his mouth and nodded like an obedient hound.

"Today, I hit my target. Twenty thousand followers. I'm a legitimate influencer now."

His reaction, this time, was less satisfactory. It took him a long, blank pause to process the words, their technicalities no doubt going somewhat over his head. Then he cleared his throat, sat up a little straighter, and finally responded: "That's good news, is it?"

"It means I'll start attracting sponsors soon. I'll be making money."

He nodded contemplatively but said nothing.

"You were worried about money, weren't you?"

His eyes widened. Like he was scared of me. I'd seen the look before: he seemed to panic at the slightest sign of my discontent. He trod cautiously, like I was some caged beast hungry for flesh and about to break free. I didn't like that he saw me that way.

"I'm happy for you," he said, diverting his eyes to a morsel of broccoli left on his plate, then swiftly sticking it in his mouth like a pacifier.

I studied the scene in front of me. The way he was sitting there, a hunched-over silhouette against the collage of wallpaper and neatly arranged furniture behind him. This was a distant picture I'd seen somewhere, on TV or in a magazine, long before I'd met Ted and made it a reality. I was deflated. This wasn't what I'd signed up for. This home I'd worked so hard to build, this life I was trying to conjure, was falling flat. I'd created the perfect backdrop. Ted was meant to leap from the canvas, bring it all to life; instead, he'd faded into the background. I'd expected more from him. Stupid. It all suddenly felt rather dramatic.

"You've killed my love," I muttered the line I was sure I'd read somewhere. It was literary. A tragic romance.

He looked at me, momentarily befuddled, then laughed. I narrowed my eyes at him, and he softened, got up from his chair and stood beside me, then stroked his fingers through my hair. Suddenly he was no longer afraid of me, humouring my rage. I didn't know which was worse. I remained stiff. He knelt down beside me and pressed my hands to his lips. A shudder ran through me.

I ripped my hands from his deceitful lips. It was suddenly so clear.

"You've killed my love." I let the force of the words shoot

through me, truer with every hair follicle they roused to attention.

"Dramatic."

He liked that word. He never used it in a sentence. It spoke for itself; so he thought. He'd grown up hearing it, no doubt. His dad probably used it to quieten his mum, his sisters, his friends throwing it back and forth in self-affirming whispers; the lie these men told themselves, that muffled and stifled the women whose honest words exposed the broken promises that proved the men had failed.

"You used to stir my imagination." I imagined my words, fluffy and bouncy and deliciously true. Like whipped cream.

Ted looked past me, of course, ever impervious to the beauty of my heartfelt revelations. It made me want to hurt him.

"You're dull, Ted."

"Sorry." His insincerity was biting.

"You might as well be dead."

He scoffed. It was all a joke to him. Our house, my cooking, my cleaning, me in my fishnets trying to make him want me. I was a joke to him. He could laugh it off and get back to his life. I was left here. All he did was laugh.

I glared at him. It felt good, knowing that I still had the power to hurt him with the intensity of a look he would never understand. Because he was too stupid, emotionally underdeveloped. I suddenly understood Medusa's wrath: her problem was never that she was cursed to turn the men she looked at to stone; the true curse was the frustration that her opponents weren't really opponents at all. A lack of true enemies can be as lonely as a lack of close friends. It can make you exceptionally existential, knowing that you'll never meet your match. Tears welled in my eyes. I was determined to stifle them.

"You used to be interested in my life. You'd ask me things."

Ted shrugged. All he did was shrug.

"You used to take me seriously."

He remained blank, blank like a boring, disappointing canvas.

"I used to believe your lies about our future."

Ted smirked. "Then we're even." He pinched my arm. "You women are all about equality, right?" He jumped up and turned to the door. Always bored of our conversations, bored of me.

"I used to believe you were man enough to make it all happen."

My last resort. Somehow the only insults that ever registered were the attacks on his masculinity. The only insults I didn't really mean. His body stiffened into that familiar shoulder square as he stood like an idiot in the doorway; the comical, the ridiculous, the hate-provoking but endearing contradiction of a man who held me hostage with his fluctuating potential to meet my needs.

"I pay for everything," he finally said.

I smirked. I'd punctured through Ted's funny. Exposed the stroppy child underneath. "The provider, really? Do you know how boring that is?"

He turned to glare at me, only spurring me on.

"I actually think I could leave you, never see you again and not care. That's how boring you are."

His shoulders drooped, both satisfying and disappointing, the familiar cocktail Ted served me in return for my efforts.

"My followers love us already, want to be us. All it would take is just a little dedication and they'd believe it, and so would you and we could be happy. But all you want to do is provide.

It's selfish, Ted. It's all about you."

I stopped. I couldn't go too far. I wanted to shake him, not push him away. And if I hadn't convinced him, I'd definitely convinced myself. It had been a pretty astonishing speech. It was clear to me: there was something important, certainly salvageable, between us. The images reflected back at me on my phone on a daily basis proved it. We were onto something. He just had to try harder.

I breathed deep and softened, raised myself from my chair – slow, deliberate – and walked over to stroke his cheek. "They could have *worshipped* us, you big dummy." I lowered my head, tried to coax his gaze from the ground, but he refused, stroppy and resolute. I cupped his chin with my hand for a while, fighting the urge suddenly to squeeze it till it burst.

"Are you happy for me at all?"

He sighed and hunched back into that deep, defeated bough shape. Then, still without lifting his eyes, he uttered the words I knew he'd been thinking all along: "It's just Instagram."

His shut his mouth. I liked that he was a coward. It made me more powerful.

"Do you know how hard I worked on this?"

"Believe me, I do."

I didn't like his tone.

"Why are you saying it like that?"

"I'm not saying it like anything."

He cleared his throat and elongated his spinal bough. Courage came to him in unconvincing bursts.

"Babe, I think you're amazing, you know that. Proper quality. You could do anything. You could get a real job. Meet some people."

I narrowed my eyes; this time, they pierced through his

thick skull, severing his condescending brain like a spit roast.

"One that pays."

"This is going to pay. It's an *unconventional* route." That word, *unconventional*, usually shut him up. Maybe because he didn't understand what it meant. Maybe because I knew I didn't really either. Either way it provided a nice dead-end to conversations when I felt cornered. But today he was defiant. He raised one sceptical eyebrow, so high I was sure he was doubting more than my chosen career path: perhaps my sanity. I was being oh-so dramatic.

"Fuck you, Ted. I didn't expect my parents to understand, but I expected you to."

His eyebrow moved even higher as if pinned to a point above his head. He was enjoying this, ridiculing me. Clearly, this had all been on his mind for some time.

"You're meant to be on my side," I said, exhausted, hoping for a reassuring hug, or at least an end to his mock defiance. But he didn't hug me. He didn't move and I didn't move because although I was disappointed, I wasn't defeated. So we stared, in suspended animation, each of us locking the other into the role of adversary; each of us waiting for some sign that the other loved us more than they wanted to prove us wrong. It was futile, we both knew, but it would take many years before I admitted that to myself. Nonetheless, that was the moment. I knew back then, right then, as I watched his eyebrow try to flee his face, that Ted had fled our picture.

SIX

I'm waiting for Ted to come home. I start on my toenails now, trimming them back so that flaky shards float on the surface of the oily water. I've always found baths stressful. Their efficacy comes down to timing. Stay in too long, and you're soaking in your own grime. To really get clean, you can't allow yourself to relax. I'm not used to maintaining this kind of focus. There isn't much space for cerebral refinement when your mind is always framing the next shot. Instagram is a full-time job. People who dismiss it as something you do in your "free time" overlook the fact that, to an influencer, all and therefore no time is free – every moment is an opportunity to rake in new followers, to post another photo, to build your brand. To be successful on IG, it has to be your life. Even now, the globules of oil are temptingly expensive-looking, gold like Christmas baubles. My hand twitches for my phone so that the clippers I am holding almost jab into my toe. I have to resist. I am Eve in the Garden of Eden. Instagram is my forbidden fruit. This time round, I will get it right.

*

The night of the chicken was the beginning of the end because it was the night that I started waiting. Waiting can take many forms. Sometimes it doesn't feel like the quiet patience of a woman at home; you might not even know you're waiting while you're fighting for a relationship to work. But you are, because you hope, and you stay, and you give, always with your eye on the horizon, on that ever-receding point where you and your loved one meet again. With a pang in my heart, I saw that night that Ted was giving up on me. It was that night, long before Tina told me to pull up my stockings and welcome my darling home, that I decided to prove to Ted that I was worth staying in the picture for. I built my Instagram, I found my followers, and I waited for him to see me. I waited for Ted, and I held on tight. I gave him another chance.

"I was actually hoping that you could help me. I could use those strong manly arms to help me pick up this chaise longue they have on hold for me at the outlet."

Ted was a simple man. Flattery was usually a reliable strategy. But today, he wasn't having any of it.

"You're buying another chair."

I was surprised that he even knew what a chaise longue was.

"It's more than a chair. It's a chaise longue." I smiled and cocked my hip coquettishly.

Ted got up from his actual chair and came and stood in front of me, his toes almost touching mine, his chin level with my forehead, his body looming tall.

"No."

I looked up, smirking, but also, strangely, a little intimidated. "Got other plans?" I tried to say breezily.

"You're not buying more furniture. Not before you're earning."

I stared at him, trying to read his face for a twitch, the suggestion of a smirk, anything to confirm my disbelief. Was he telling me what to do? He remained stoic.

"It's not really up to you," I said, waving my hand to indicate how easily I could dismiss him. "It's my money."

"It's your dad's money," he growled, still so close to my face I could smell remnants of kebab masking after-work pints on his breath.

"Does it matter where it came from? It's mine now."

"You said you wanted to stop freeloading."

"It's a gift, not freeloading. There is a difference."

He arched his neck and exhaled, bull-like. I suddenly understood.

"OK, darling."

He stopped short, his scowl dropping into dumbfounded confusion. Back to the Ted I knew. "What?"

"Yes, I understand, darling. You want me to hold off until I'm contributing to the household."

I came up behind him, then placed my hands on his shoulders and pushed him back down to seated. I massaged his thick neck.

"You work so hard."

He looked up at me all puppy-like. Peace had been restored. I kissed his cheek, then cleared the table, wiped it clean, and pulled him onto the dishcloth-damp wood.

"My stallion," I whispered in his ear and his nostrils flared. I turned onto my front and presented him with his final serving of plump flesh. He grabbed my buttocks and squeezed hard, digging his fingertips deep into the cellulite segments, then parted them like a peach and entered me.

I plotted as he pounded. Of course, I was still going to buy the chaise longue. It was just a matter of how and when. Of how to sneak it past his fragile ego. That was part of being a girl-friend. This I knew even before Tina had taught me anything at all.

I decided that his family would be the buffer. They didn't like me. But they humoured me. Which I was starting to think was the most I could ever expect from the people who, despite our shared nationality, would always be foreigners to me. To them, too, I was strange. A quaint curiosity that Ted had picked up from a village fete and now kept in his house. They did – they thought he "kept" me, like "Kiera Knightley in one of them costume dramas or summat". The "posh girl" who may have left her cushy life but, they warned, would always "expect" things. Ted didn't contradict them, never told them that the truth of our relationship was that I didn't need him but that I'd chosen him – voluntarily. That somehow devalued him as a person, he must have thought.

"You'll never be one of them," Dad told me the day I announced I was moving out of the house and in with Ted.

"How do you know? It's not like you've ever tried," I'd hurled back and immediately regretted it.

Dad had always been arrogant, but it wasn't his fault. Privilege had made him that way. He was rooted in a time and place, and he'd never been shown a way out. Things were different for me. The world was connected now in ways he wouldn't ever be able to assimilate into his cemented worldview. My Instagram following was composed of the daughters of Saudi oligarchs, American interior designers and British middle-income stay-at-home mothers. Class the way he knew it was a meaningless myth in the modern world. He'd looked a little shaken by my viciousness; his little girl may not always have agreed with him, but she had always stayed affectionate. He deserved that much.

"Sorry, Daddy," I'd told him. I'd hugged him and told him I'd still come to visit. Only I never did, because that would have meant confronting a reality far too dangerous in the midst of my struggle: that Dad was right.

In any case, Ted's façade gave me leverage. If it was so important to him that his family believed that he was the all-saying breadwinner, the last thing he'd want them to think was that I was making a mockery of him. He'd want them to think that he had control in how I spent the money he gener-ously bestowed on me. It would be embarrassing for him to admit that I'd defied him, that I'd gone and spent my pocket money on forbidden sweets. I would buy the chaise longue and invite his family for tea on the day it arrived. Ted would have to play it cool, wouldn't want to confront me until they'd left, by which point his family's approval of the chair would have placated him. We'd always shared a commitment to domestic professionalism, you see. His image, which depended on our image, mattered to him. Just as much as it did to me. It was one of the few things that truly bound us.

SEVEN

I'm waiting for Ted to come home. It is time for the assault. I pluck, scrape and grate. I shave my legs, armpits, even between my legs – back to front. I file all my nails: fingers and toes. I scrub my back, pumice my feet, tweeze every last nipple hair I can find. When I feel I've done all I can, I lift myself out of the human soup of a bath, by now definitely past its expiration date, and stand swaying on the spot, dizzy as the blood drains from my boiling head.

Slowly, consciousness descends on me. It's clear to me now: my body has been crying out for years, I'd just been too stubborn to listen. I'd convinced myself that pining would fix things, that manifesting my sadness would drive Ted to take it seriously. But Tina had made me see. To Ted, my strike had looked like indifference. He saw a woman disappointed with her life, and so with him. A woman who had stopped making the effort. It was selfish, what I'd done. I'd been so fixated on making him see me, that I'd stopped doing anything to deserve it. What I thought had been determination was actually retreat, fortification inside the folds of my flaky, itchy skin. I dry myself off and lather myself in lotion.

*

Tina must have seen it coming. She'd been there from the beginning of the end. The day I brought the chaise longue home, a spring day, birds chirping, air soft and full of promise, she was there. She'd been standing in her front garden, perfectly made up, of course, and wearing a glorious red-and-gold embroidered kaftan, when the van had pulled up at the house, and had remained, watching, as I'd emerged and ushered in the men I'd paid to transport the illicit acquisition. I'd been hesitant to walk outside, desperate to lay my eyes on the trophy, of course, but keen to avoid the judgemental gazes of the neighbours who bore witness to my frequent expenditures.

Tina had approached me as I'd stood cowering on the edge of the pavement, the jingling of bangles and hoops announcing an intervention.

"You saw fit to make another purchase, my dear?"

I looked up and into her emerald eyes outlined with chalky grey.

"It's quite lovely. I think you'd like it."

"And what is Ted's stance on the matter?"

She peered at me over the edge of her moon-frame glasses. She already knew.

"He hasn't seen it yet."

Her nostrils flared as she exhaled, announcing exhaustion-fuelled crabbiness.

"Recalcitrance. You're like the part of a fossil that resists decomposition. Your entire generation just a collection of crustaceans set into rock. It is the flesh that matters. The flesh that runs warm with a man's touch. The flesh that dimples as he presses his fingers into you."

I was trying to listen, but I had to make sure the chaise would make it in one piece. I flinched as I saw one of the men stumble on the kerb. Tina swished her hand in front of my face.

"You are living in reverse, preserving a life that is yet to be lived." Her voice was thin and sharp like a fishbone. Disguised in the richness of shimmering flesh, she pierced your throat as you swallowed her words whole.

"Now, you must remember, men are easily disquieted. You mustn't make him feel like a stranger in his own home."

I stared down at my toes like a naughty schoolchild.

"He doesn't care, really, not about the furniture," I said. "He just doesn't like me doing my own thing."

"And you think that's ridiculous?" Tina's reptilian eyes flared, making clear the only permissible answer.

"It's a bit old-fashioned, don't you think?" I was playing with dragon fire.

Tina tutted, but I seemed to have a suicide wish.

"I know what you're going to say. That it's my job to make him feel like a man, or whatever. Thing is, I've got better things to be doing."

Tina looked at me, letting her unwavering silence do the work. I clenched my fists, bracing myself for her wrath. I watched her thin lips and imagined the flames they'd spew.

When she finally opened her mouth, her thin voice was clear and steady. "And you think that's ridiculous?"

This time, I bit my tongue. She paused, then turned towards her house.

"Follow me."

I looked over my shoulder at the workers now wrestling the chaise longue through the doorway.

"Now," Tina ordered, waving a wiry hand through the air.

I followed her into the house.

"Sit down." Tina pointed to my usual armchair by the fireplace. I sat down, both curious and pre-emptively nostalgic. Something told me that, by the time we were done, that chair would never seem quite so inviting again.

I loved Tina's house for the same reason that it terrified me – nothing ever changed. Her trinkets forever fixed to their spots; even the ones I'd never seen before I knew had always been there. It was comfortable because it was familiar, and it was petrifying, quite literally, because it didn't allow you to reinvent or replenish. It didn't allow you to forget, and so it didn't allow you to change.

Tina disappeared behind a Japanese room divider and returned in a flash carrying a teapot already steaming and full. As if she'd planned it. She poured some into my usual china cup, the one with the snakes on it that she knew I liked, and handed it to me before taking her own cup to her usual spot on an antique bamboo chair across from me. She brought the cup to her face, letting the fumes fog up her lenses, fully aware that she was leaving me in suspense.

"Nothing better to put an end to the self-pity of a lost generation than a story of true hardship. I've been meaning to tell you the story of how Stanley and I met."

Stanley – she'd never used his name before. It was rare for her to disclose details of any kind. She preferred abstractions over anecdote, spoke in the kinds of quotations you were meant to find on dusty scrolls or fortune cookies, their meaning only emerging over the course of a life.

"I suppose I was waiting for the right moment, waiting for you to find the humility required for any form of self-improvement. But I see now that that was wishful thinking."

I nodded, understanding only that she had insulted me, and that I probably deserved it. She cleared her throat, softly, but with purpose, her lenses finally starting to clear, the green of her eyes – I now saw – swirling with amber and black.

"We were both young when we met. Not that young, of course, not like the youth of today." She took the opportunity to sneer at me. "Germany had ruined him, you see. That's what he always said. It hadn't, of course. The war only made him stronger. People used to be resilient like that. But his circumstances were tragic."

She paused for a moment, lost in thought, biting her lip as she remembered her long-departed love. Life was so lonely. I didn't want to be old.

"He'd returned to a wife who had fallen pregnant in his absence. The child, it later emerged, belonged to one of the lodgers at the guesthouse she ran in London. On hearing of the inconvenience, this new acquaintance had hung himself on the bedpost of room number two, his regular room for the duration of their affair."

A child, to Tina – an inconvenience. I shuddered at the thought of the kind of love story this would be.

"Stanley was put in an unfortunate position, feeling obligated to provide for a woman who had cuckolded him. But he stuck by her; of course he did. People used to have integrity. He told me it was duty that made him stay, but I know it was sympathy, too. He'd seen too much loss during the war to permit himself to be the cause of another. People used to have compassion."

"What happened to the baby?"

"He was eventually relieved of his fate, although I know he didn't see it that way, when she died in childbirth. He met me not long after that."

I watched her sip her tea, as engrossed in her own story as I was.

"The best love stories start with people at a crossroads. People seeking change are open to the kind of personal evolution required to forge a bond. Personal evolution of course has become extinct in your time. He came to me for a tarot card reading."

"You were a fortune-teller?"

"I don't believe in denominations. Your generation seems to be obsessed with them. People came to me with questions. I found a way to answer them."

"And people believed you?"

Tina leaned forward on her bamboo scaffold, the wood squeaking, puffing out the musty scent of dust.

"Now, listen. The war taught us humility. No one would have predicted the utter devastation it caused."

"Not even a fortune-teller?"

Tina sighed, and the wry smirk drained from my face. I felt empty. Something had made me suddenly obstinate. Perhaps it was that I was disappointed; now that I knew she was a kook, she'd lost at least some of her credibility.

"Your generation equates belief with ignorance. The unknown, my dear, is the only certainty you'll ever have."

It wasn't fair. Tina got to lecture me on humbling myself while she got to unlock the secrets of the universe.

"What makes you so confident, Tina?"

She nodded, acknowledging something that wasn't my question.

"Funny, really. When Stanley came to me, he said that I reminded him of the women he'd shared beds with during the war. Women who, given the uncertainty of tomorrow, never expected more than a night."

"Don't need wartime conditions for that. Try Tinder."

Tina swept one kimono-shaped sleeve through the air, dismissing my insolence. She raised her voice. "He was speaking of the honesty of a moment allowed to exist in suspension. Your world demands resolution. You want your happy endings, endings you think you already deserve. Stanley knew, and I understood, that stories have to be written."

She sipped her tea, and continued to speak past me, as if to someone behind me. I shuddered as imagined it was Stanley dressed in his khakis.

"It's the great nuisance of this mortal existence that it takes the threat of nihilation to force us to live. It saddens me that death doesn't exist for your generation. In any case, I told Stanley his fate, and then he told me that he wanted me in it."

She swished the no doubt now lukewarm jasmine tea in her mouth, enjoying the poignancy of the sweet leaves, along with that of her words. Age did have its perks. I wanted to bask in my own wisdom.

"Young women today spend too much time thinking about what men see in them. Stanley was the first man not to see me as a witch, but as a woman. That's why I chose him. But when I married him, I vowed forever to do him the same justice, by seeing him first as a person, then as a man. And so I chose him every day, for the person he was, and not the person he saw in me."

She was a woman, but also a witch. I had to be wary of the spells she was trying to cast on me.

"What are you telling me to do?" I asked.

"It's no easy vow to keep, my dear. For me, it meant forgiveness, even as the shadows of his past possessed him to do me unthinkable harm. When his demons defiled my body, I remembered that he was first and foremost a human carrying pain, only momentarily the man who violated me. That allowed me to love him, even then, and that allowed us to move past that unfortunate incident."

I shuddered.

"Throw out the idea of the person you are living with. Ted doesn't owe you anything you don't deserve."

I'd had enough of Tina's lessons. They were disturbing. And boring. Almost as boring as Ted.

"Tina?"

She'd presented me with a much more interesting possibility.

"Would you do a tarot reading for me?"

I watched her put down her cup and smack her wet lips.

"That, coincidentally, is why you're here."

EIGHT

I'm waiting for Ted to come home. I've turned to my face. I pluck the stray hairs from around my eyebrows until they form perfect arches, just like Tina's. I apply layer after layer of anti-wrinkle ointment until my skin shines, now visibly smoother, if not as taut as I'd hoped. I have to be realistic; I'm not going to reverse the signs of ageing. But that doesn't matter. True confidence means accepting your age, "ageing gracefully", like Tina. No Botox required. It's more about making the effort; that's what Ted needs to see. Relationships are all about gestures, however empty. It's about showing him that you care for yourself, because you love yourself, so that he will want to love you too. Exuding confidence was what made the man swoon. And now, I was ready.

The best love stories start with people at a crossroads. I think back to Tina's words. Only now do I understand what they mean, what it really feels like to give yourself to love. Perhaps I've aged more gracefully than I thought – I am wiser.

Tina pulled out a small, polished oak coffee table, then disappeared behind the room divider and returned carrying an assortment of objects wrapped in magenta silk. She unwrapped them and draped the cloth over the table. Then, she turned to the other items: a few sticks of sandalwood, a plate and a polished black box. She sat down, her kaftan parting slightly, then perched the box on her bony kneecaps. Next, with trance-like ease, she took one of the wood pieces and in one swift motion stuck one end in the fireplace and then extracted it masterfully without as much as singeing her hand. She held the stick up, letting the smoke fill the room with its hypnotic earthiness. She placed it down and let it smoulder on the plate, then turned her attention to the box, stroking it with her gangly fingers, readying herself for what was inside. She lifted the lid. I leaned over to peek inside, but she slammed the box shut.

"Stay away!" She took a breath to compose herself. "Stay away from the cards."

I glued my back to the chair.

"You must listen, follow my lead. Questions will only curtail the inevitable, disrupt the forces that can destroy us with ease. This isn't a personality quiz in the *Cosmopolitan*, Rosalind. It will be a challenge for you to imagine – it always is for your generation – that this procedure isn't actually about you."

"Procedure?" This sounded alarmingly clinical. Visions of wartime surgeries, of shiny scalpels and dispensable lives. Tina, the woman who saw babies as inconveniences, deaths as merely unfortunate. I didn't believe in magic, but I believed in skewed priorities. Had I invited a madwoman to disrupt the most intimate parts of my life?

"This is a blueprint, a constellation on which you are a pinprick, a speck." Tina snapped her fingers close to my face, which was crumpled with doubt. "Don't for a second think this makes you the centre of the universe."

I looked at the hand covered in age-spots that had just brought me back into the room, then at her face, her placid, bloodhound's face. I was just humouring an old lady, doing her a favour. She wasn't dangerous. She was kooky, and she was lonely. And I was doing this for her.

"I want you to remember that it is for you to navigate your way through the complexities of space and time. All I can hope to do is channel the forces that encapsulate you. I can offer you a way into the vortex, but you will never be in control. Youngsters today are such control freaks."

Control freak. It didn't sound right coming from Tina. It was one of those small lapses that reminded me that Tina did, after all, occupy my present, that she wasn't just an illusion I'd conjured up in my mind. Freaks, in her time, I imagined, were the people you'd see at a circus. Bearded women and elasticated men. Back then, you kept them at bay. Control freaks would have faded in comparison with the caged freaks they had to gawk over. Perhaps, I suddenly thought, Tina could be my freak, caged conveniently in the house next door, reminding me every day that there were truly deluded people. But then her dragon's glare reminded me who was in control. I nodded with all the sombre gravity I knew she expected.

"Fine," she said, reopening the box. She closed her eyes, hovering her hands over the cards, then picking them up and feathering them out in front of me, inviting me to choose one.

"Point! Don't touch."

I pointed and she laid the card on the cloth, repeating the process nine times until three rows of cards were spread out across the table.

We took them in together, watching them as if they might come to life.

"It is important to sit with the cards, to let their meaning diffuse."

I nodded, again, to please her.

She closed her eyes once more. Then, her lizardy eyelid flicked open and she flipped the first card.

"This is your past and your significator." She studied the card. "The Three of Wands." She'd closed her eyes again. I guessed she was still letting the meaning "diffuse". "You are letting life pass you by, missing the world and all the good things it has to offer. Perhaps, it is possible, that this orientation has brought rewards, but now it has left you stranded. It has made you obsolete."

Obsolete. My heart rumbled. Was my Instagram doomed to fail? Did Tina realise what curse she was projecting? That obsolescence was the modern-day equivalent of death?

She looked up from the cards, unaffected by my wide-eyed terror. "Tell me, Rosalind, are you weary?"

I definitely felt older. "Relationships can be tiring." I offered it like an excuse.

"Yes, it must be tiring, for your generation, to have to compromise your selfishness."

I huffed.

"What you perceive to be the consequences of some sort of inhumane sacrifice, my dear, might just be wear-and-tear, might just be your own sense of life passing you by."

My eyes drifted back to the cards. I wanted reassurance, not more of her sexist mantras.

"Seize your fate, Rosalind!" She lifted her arms and cupped her fists as if she was grabbing two imperceptible balls, perhaps Stanley's testicles, from the air. It was all very exhausting.

She looked at me like she wanted to shake me. I stayed

still. Eventually she gave up and continued to move through the cards. I faded out as she rambled on in her vague generalities. I thought of Mother, who had always indulged a "guilty pleasure" for horoscopes. Guilty, because she had to hide them from Dad. Horoscopes "niggled" him. God forbid that my dad felt "niggled", a word that never quite captured the toxicity that suffused the house and everyone in it when he did. It was just Dad, just his reaction to a "mind-numbing, self-indulgent, utterly tasteless predilection to believing what you want to believe".

"Women need too much assurance, that was the real problem," he'd say.

Dad was wrong. Tina's reading wasn't reassuring. Not even helpful. She had by now moved on from my past to my present. She flipped another card.

"As expected, The Hermit. Reversed."

I rolled my eyes.

She lifted her chin and peered down at me. "Your home is very cosy, isn't it?"

"I'm not a hermit, Tina. My home is not just a home, it's my studio. It's where I create interiors. Have I shown you my Instagram?"

Tina raised her chin even higher. "But you are hiding."

I wanted to hide. From her, and her ridiculous expectations. I didn't venture out much, that was true, but people did that less as they settled down and grew up. I was doing exactly what she kept pushing me to do. I was committing to the life I'd chosen. What more did she expect?

"I've been trying to build a life," I mumbled, feebly.

She pursed her lips and threw me an infuriatingly sceptical side-glare. "I do sympathise. It must be difficult, having chosen for an honest life, to face the world out there. You must struggle at times to know what to do. To know what's right."

I knew I'd sensed a snake. She'd lured me in here to do Ted's bidding, to convince me to send the chaise longue back and give up my Instagram. Because, just like Ted, she didn't understand. She was too old to see. Mistook what I was doing for a horoscope, that I was trying to nestle myself in the illusion of certainty, in a world I could control. I wasn't hiding. Instagram was the real world now. I was putting myself out there, several times a day, taking risks. Building a brand. The work I was doing was just imperceptible to her; it existed in a virtual dimension this particular psychic couldn't see.

"I'm not scared, Tina," I said, in a tone steady like stone. "I'm taking risks in a world you don't understand."

Tina snorted.

"I have a following."

"A following, they call it! Like you're some visionary. I'm sure they're all deeply committed to your profound doctrine, but I wasn't talking about your Instagram, darling. I was talking about your relationship."

I groaned. "Does everything always have to be about Ted? Have you even heard of the Bechdel test?"

Tina erupted into a maniacal cackle. "You mean the ridiculous premise that refusing to discuss the thing that matters to us most, our hearts, is a sign of emancipation? Yes, I've heard of that particular joke poisoning the young women of our time."

I'd been mistaken. Tina wasn't timeless after all. She was a dinosaur. *She* was the real relic in this room.

"Yes, well, I'm sorry that you resent young women for having the rights you didn't." I said. "I'm sorry that we get to put our own careers first."

"You don't want a career. You're a love-first girl."

I shot up from my seat, almost knocking over the coffee table as I did. The cards scattered across the floor. I turned to leave.

Tina stayed seated and silent. She only spoke when I opened the door. "I'll leave the cards here. We'll move on to your future when you're ready."

I looked over my shoulder at her narrow, immobilised body. I wouldn't be coming back.

NINE

I'm waiting for Ted to come home. I check the clock on the wall. It's five past seven. Although he's not as reliable as he used to be, he'll be home soon. Better get ready. I have to make him feel welcome in his own home. That's the most important thing, Tina had always said. What better way to turn a fresh leaf than to repurpose the symbolic heart of our differences, the chaise longue?

I remember an old joke Dad had once told at a dinner party. In it, a woman had performed the self-same ritual I had. Dad must have over-indulged on the digestifs, because the joke had escalated into the kind of raunchiness he usually reserved for his male friends – still audible to all the women, of course, as his voice cascaded through the halls from his office where the men would sit throwing back whisky and puffing cigars. In the joke he told that day to scandalously mixed company, the woman, just like me, had readied herself for her husband's return, bathing and cleansing and perfuming. Then, she'd spread herself naked on the sofa, presenting herself to her husband when he got home. When, shocked by the full-frontal display, he asked her what she was doing, she told him she'd donned her "love dress" for him. To which he replied: "Needs ironing."

I remember how angry I'd been at my dad for telling it. Typical of a man of his generation, to have so limited an imagination as to think that a woman left alone for a few hours could think of nothing better than to seduce her husband, I'd told him, while being distinctly aware that we were having the kind of debate better fitted to a Jane Austen novel than the present day. "It's just a joke," he'd said. Now I see that it wasn't. That all of Dad's jokes were depressingly real.

I'm terrified that Ted will tell me to iron my love dress. But Tina had told me to be brave. I've learnt from my mistakes. Hermit no longer, my body will be a peace offering served on our chaise longue. I will welcome him home, the way I used to in the early days, but this time, utterly selfless.

I make my way downstairs, completely naked, and stop in front of the curvaceous beauty. Still so elegant after all these years. I approach it, cautiously, as if it is a wild animal, moving around it to take in its form, calibrating how it will merge with my own. Once I've sufficiently apprehended my opponent, I lower my bum onto the velvet padding. I exhale as my body melts onto the seat.

The woodwork was impeccable, smooth like freshly shaven legs, I observed after returning from my botched tarot reading. I'd paid the workers extra, apologising for my extended absence, then channelled all the rage Tina had incited into tearing open the tight plastic wrapping. I took in the delicate wisps and twirls of the carving, the gloss of the polish, so soft on the eyes it almost made you drowsy. Tina had tried to divert me from my course, but I was right to trust my impulses. This was a solid buy.

I'd always wanted a chaise longue. They were utterly impractical, and that made them sexy. Mum had always had one in her bedroom. She never let me sit on it because it was an antique. To which I'd always respond that she was too, the retort I probably learned from Dad. Then she'd push me out of the room, and spend an extra twenty minutes powdering her nose – not figuratively, Mum actually used white powder because foundation was "vulgar", by which she meant afford-able, by which she meant that a person's value was commen-surate with the cost of the luxury items they coated them-selves in.

In any case, this chaise longue was mine to do with as I pleased. But it wasn't just for me. The "chair", as Ted had so dismissively called it, represented the kind of life he and I would have together. One in which we prioritised hedonistic impulses over quotidian concerns like the need to sit comfort-ably. Once he found a way to put his ego aside, he would see that this was an investment in *our* future.

I wasted no time and called Wendy, his mother, inviting her over for the evening of the day the chaise longue had arrived. I knew she'd jump at the chance for a visit, given that Ted never made the effort with her and he was her favourite. I knew her husband, Tony, wouldn't come – he had nightly obligations involving his "mates" and "footie". I told Wendy she should invite Ted's sisters, Nancy and Amy, on my behalf. I never liked calling them directly. We didn't have much to talk about.

The doorbell rang at 6:30, as instructed, giving me time to get them enthused about my new furniture before Ted got home. The three women stood on my doorstep, shifting, adjusting their clothes, always slightly uncomfortable in my presence. They assumed that I, being "posh", cared what they looked like, and so always talked about "making an effort" for their visits, while obviously resenting me for it.

"Lovely to see you all!" I screeched, frighteningly friendly.

They all smiled stiffly, then followed me into the lounge.

"Please, sit down," I tried to say more calmly. They looked around the room, surveying their options. I watched as their eyes scanned first the lounge set, then moved to the corner where I'd put the chaise longue, visibly confused about where to sit, but too afraid to ask, lest there was some kind of posh girl etiquette they were unaware of. I grinned to myself and turned to the kitchen, waiting for them to pluck up the courage to treat me like family instead of the Queen Mother for once.

Only Nancy, the youngest and bravest, dared to speak: "Where d'you want us?"

I casually looked over my shoulder from my place at the countertop.

"Why don't we try out the new seat I bought," I said, opting for lay terms, not wanting to alienate them with the French the chaise longue really deserved.

They made their way obediently to the far corner while I made the tea. When I turned to carry the tray to them, they were still hovering in front of it.

"Please, sit!"

They lowered their bottoms hesitantly onto the seat, perching barely on the edge. I set the tray down on the coffee table I'd put there in anticipation.

"Is it comfortable? I just got it today."

"It's nice," Nancy said.

I poured the tea and handed them a cup each. I watched them sip in silence, searching for my next move.

"I do like to spruce up the house. You understand, don't you ladies?"

They all nodded in unison.

"How's the garden, Wendy?"

"Alright," she said, lowering her gaze to her cup, and then dragging it back up. "When does Ted get home?"

I sighed. It was as if hiding your discomfort was a skill only cultivated by the upper classes. I watched Wendy for a while. There was always something compressed about her, her neck merging with her body. She resembled a badger, or a mole.

"Shouldn't be long now. He's been working late recently."

The women all glanced at each other knowingly. Like they knew about our problems. Like it was my fault.

"How's Tony?" I fired.

Wendy's eyes narrowed. This wasn't going well. I needed them sweet before Ted got home.

"Dad's always the same," Amy said, gloriously oblivious to the subtext. Amy was about twenty-five, the middle child, but she could have been anywhere between fifteen and thirty-five. There was something almost subconscious about her, a total lack of animation or drive, that made her seem both juvenile and wise at the same time.

"Consistent," I said, thankful to her in any case for providing a cue. "Like father, like son, it seems. Ted doesn't like too much upheaval. He isn't a fan of change."

Wendy softened, smiling. "Teddy was always a creature of habit. Liked his toys and his telly, that's it. Lovely lad."

I nodded. "Yes, always takes a bit of convincing, even with the small things. Like new furniture."

Wendy's head shot up. Like she knew. Ted had probably talked to her. Perhaps I'd underestimated him.

A key in the lock. My pulse short-circuited.

"He's here!" Wendy shot up.

Amy and Nancy reclined, suddenly more at ease.

I listened as Ted plodded, as always, into the hall, taking his time to hang up his coat, as always, like he was stalling for time. Wendy was impatient. She walked into the hall to greet him.

"Surprise!" I heard her say, followed by the squelch of sloppy lips on cheek.

"What're you doing here, Mums?" he said, about as unimpressed as I'd expected.

"An impromptu visit," I interjected, my hysterically upbeat voice returning.

Ted entered the room, his mum hanging from his arm.

He noticed the chaise longue before he did his sisters.

"You got it. After I told you not to."

I looked up at him, trying not to look guilty. I hadn't factored in this degree of brazenness.

Wendy looked down at me from her spot next to Ted, clearly enjoying the altercation. I glanced over at Nancy and Amy, trying to ascertain their loyalties, but they looked blank, useless.

"Let's talk about it later," was the best I could come up with. "Tea?" I quickly poured the already over-brewed dark brown tea into my own cup, handed it to him on a saucer. He stared at it, the pink and gold china hovering in front him, looking feeble, like a child-sized cupcake being offered to a cannibal. Wendy and the girls watched, their necks all extended in a row, heads all turned towards him in transparent glee.

Perhaps it was their obnoxiousness that saved me. He looked at them, rolled his eyes. He wasn't going to give them a show. He took the cup. I exhaled, fractionally.

"Make space for Teddy bear." Wendy nudged Nancy who

bumped Amy so that they all shifted down the chaise longue. Wendy patted the space beside her. "Come sit with yer mum."

My jaw clenched. He looked like a bulldog, squeezed into his dark blue suit, shoulder pads straining, white belly exposed in his shirt that gaped at the apex of his gut, his legs funny and small beneath his big flank, pretty pink teacup perching daintily in one hand.

He sighed and sank down beside his mum. I rolled my shoulders, releasing the tension, preparing for the next hurdle. I pulled up a stool and sat down across from the row of kin.

"We really should do this more often," I spoke into the silence. They all looked at me with paralytic faces, a strain of unimpressed that must have been genetic.

"It's what this home is for, after all: family," I tried again. "Ted and I are just trying to build a home to share and enjoy. Life's too short not to have those moments, don't you think?"

I scratched my head.

"Mum's been busy. Loads of cleaning," Amy said while reaching for some shortbread from the tray. Nancy slapped her hand away.

"No, please. I forgot to offer!" I screeched, so grateful to have an occupation that I shoved the plate a bit too forcefully in Amy's direction. She shrugged and took a handful of biscuits.

Ted hadn't noticed the feeble display. "You're cleaning again, Mum?"

Wendy glared at Amy like she might back-hand her. It wouldn't surprise me if she had. She was a distastefully aggressive woman.

"Don't you be worrying about me, Teddy dear. I'm a tough old bird, like yer dad always says." She nudged him playfully in his side.

He frowned, then looked at me, as if deciding whether or not to let me in on intimate family business. "Is Dad on the dole again?"

Wendy huffed and stared sourly ahead, like a schoolgirl in trouble, a strange sight, with the tuft of grey sprouting from her head, her leathery smoker's complexion, her wiry arms always strained for a fight. Ted looked luscious and meaty and warm in comparison. He wrapped one arm around her. I was proud of him.

"His back's givin' out, that's all. Luggin' bricks at his age. But he'll be back on his feet, love, don't ya worry." She reached a cigarette-stained hand to pat his face, but she couldn't bring herself to look at him. She was ashamed, I noticed for the first time. They all were. Ted was too.

"It's actually more because he drinks gallons." Nancy's thin voice pierced through the heavy silence.

"Shut yer mouth," Wendy snapped.

Ted looked at me self-consciously and sighed. He pulled his mother in closer.

"You have to be honest with me, OK, Mums. You know I can help."

"She don't take help from no one." The words fell out of Amy's mouth along with crumbs of biscuit.

I took it all in. It wasn't what I'd imagined when I'd bought the chaise longue, but it looked surprisingly picturesque, the sad family atop the crushed velvet, against the appliqué florals of wallpaper and mahogany ornaments. Rather like a painting, the same melancholy as that of a demure damsel in a Victorian domestic scene.

The whole saga had distracted Ted beautifully. Perhaps it had even done the work for me. The sentimental memory would subconsciously forge a bond to the new furniture. Men's emotions were simple like that. The chair would suddenly feel right to him and he wouldn't even be able to explain why.

I let the family sit there, the bonds between them and the love seat holding them, forging them together in compassionate silence. Ted finally patted his mother's back and cleared his throat.

"We'll sort ya out, alright? Don't you worry." He looked at me, ordering me to agree.

"That's right, Wendy. We're family now, really. We're there for you." I reached over and put my hand on her knee. Ted watched, slightly uncomfortably, but then noticing his mum's lack of resistance, seemed satisfied. I'd done my duty.

I stayed there, in the affectionate pose I had appropriately chosen, letting my eyes scan the row, trying to read the room. Was this the opportune moment?

I hesitated, then cleared my throat, speaking ever so softly, lightly, like a sensitive, caring girlfriend – dare I say, even a wife – would do. "It's like I was saying before, we want to share everything we have with you. And so, when I buy things, I buy them to enjoy together. It's not just for me, or my Instagram; it's all for you too."

My eyes set on Ted. Had I struck the right chord? I watched him. There was an almost imperceptible nod as he processed my words, reflecting, no doubt, on their considerate poignancy. I watched him, his eyes moving slowly, steadily, up to meet mine. Then a pause.

A bitesize teacup hit the floor. Smashing china shattered the silence.

"For the love of–" Ted shot up, a dark bough arching over me. "This isn't about you, alright?"

I panicked, looking around, at Amy, mid-bite; at Nancy, eyes wide; Wendy, smirking.

"I know it's not," I stuttered. "I was just trying to–"

"I know exactly what you were trying to do, and I'm not having it, alright?"

"Ted, I didn't mean anything by it."

"You can't help yourself, can ya? Did you hear Mum just now? We have real problems, you selfish bitch."

"Ted, language, please." I looked over at Wendy. Her tiny little mole eyes sparkled.

Ted moved towards me. "Can you ever just drop the bloody furniture thing?"

"I really don't feel comfortable discussing this when we have company," I tried to say, smiling, sounding uncannily like my own mother.

"Tough tits," said Ted, sounding uncannily like his own father.

Amy snorted. Nancy elbowed her in the ribs. The room fell silent.

Ted finally sunk back down, dropped his face to his palms and groaned, "I'm so tired of this."

"I did warn ya," Wendy mumbled, loud enough for us all to hear.

They'd been talking. It all made sense now. Ted's recent obstinacy. Putting his foot down at dinner. Now this. Who else would have inspired such defiance but the former woman in his life, the one who had always felt threatened by the posh tart who stole her son away?

Why were women always making things difficult? My father's voice echoed through my skull, always annoyingly present, increasingly a reality I couldn't deny. It was so clear to me now. It was all Wendy's fault. She'd said it herself: Ted was sweet-natured. It wouldn't have occurred to him to form an opinion, let alone resist any of my decisions. She'd corrupted him. The whole emotional melodrama she'd just staged, probably part of her plan to push me out. Behind every mediocre man is a woman telling him what to do. I had to be that woman.

I stood up. "Wendy, I don't think this is really any of your business."

Wendy's head retracted further into her flabby neck. I wished it would disappear.

"My son is my business." She clenched her fists and leaned forward, instantly reanimated after her fragile old woman act. "Tell her, doll, tell her what you said. Family first."

"Who's making him choose?" I shouted, voice cracking, composure lost. I looked deep into Ted's twitching eye-slits, daring him to confirm what I already knew.

He looked back, shifting, reassuringly, still palpably scared of me.

Unfortunately, Wendy wasn't. "Tell 'er, Ted. Tell 'er you ain't happy."

"Mum, calm down." Ted looked down at the floor, avoiding both of our gazes. He was caught between his two "number one lasses", as he liked to call us. Maybe he did feel torn, but he didn't look like someone deciding between two people, he looked like someone who didn't feel he deserved either. I watched him looking boyish. It was that vulnerability that used to make me melt, that used to wash away the aftertaste of his so-called banter, the sexist jokes and dismissiveness. Watching those bashful bug eyes evade my own used to remind me that he meant well. He was just a boy, underneath it all, the boy who always thought that because I was rich, I was better than him.

The boy who believed that he was still winning me over. The boy who had to gather all his confidence to risk pushing me away to stand his ground. However misguided, I would always think, he was doing what he thought was right.

Only, now, childish Ted wasn't endearing but disappointing. He wasn't enough. He had to grow up. I didn't want a child; I wanted husband material. I didn't want to compete with his mother, because I wasn't his mother. I was supposed to be the love of his life, *his* Stepford wife.

"I'm bored of this, Ted. Say what you want to say."

"I, uh…" He couldn't do it. He didn't have it in him to stand up for himself.

"I've never been less attracted to you than I am right now." Those words would sting. I wanted them to. But I said them to test myself as much as him. I wanted to see if I still cared.

His head drooped even lower, and I felt it, that indispensable feeling you forget sometimes when you live with someone you're supposed to love – sympathy. It was still there, and I was relieved. Without it we didn't stand a chance.

"Ted, let's just forget it all and move on, OK?" I leaned over and held his face with both hands.

He looked up at me. I glanced at Wendy, who was already bitter about her imminent defeat. That was the way it was meant to be. I was the one he wanted. He'd fallen in love with the posh girl with the sexy chaise longue and the decent ass, and there was no going back.

"We can ignore the chair, Ted. It doesn't matter."

Ted's head shot up. His little black beads turned to fiery red. "No. We can't."

I jolted, shocked by his devilish anger. It wasn't like him. It wasn't him. He was possessed. Even Wendy froze, gathering herself for all of two seconds before she moved in on the beast, knowing it would be worth the risk if it meant destroying me.

"Tell 'er, Teddy bear!" she hissed close to his ear.

Ted shrugged her off and stood up. He looked us all up and down, as if, suddenly, we were all alike, all members of the same inferior species, all just biding our time before he decided our fate. He breathed, sucking in all the air in the room, leaving us all on the verge of choking.

The red in his eyes settled, turning first to orange, then yellow, then black. He gave us our oxygen.

"It's me or the chair, Rosie." His thin little lips quivered but he stood his ground. "It's time I got some respect around 'ere."

"Really?" I tried to say, choking on my attempt at a snigger. It wasn't funny. It was terrifying.

TEN

I'm waiting for Ted to come home. I've timed my ritual perfectly. I'm all but ready for him, the picture almost done; all that is left to do is to find the perfect composition. I extend my arms above my head and point my now perfectly painted toes, channelling Kate Winslet in *Titanic*. It takes me a while to balance aesthetics against comfort, the latter of which I have decided since buying the chaise longue is actually essential, but eventually I settle into my pose. Now I have to wait.

I have a perfect view of the clock on the wall, the clock I'd picked up from the outlet one Boxing Day while Ted was at the pub. I watch the dials tick in slow motion past the comically large numbers. The wait is going to be more difficult than I thought. I'm struck suddenly by the considerable urge to photograph the scene I'm in. It's quite romantic. My arm: soft, dainty, delicate, draped over the edge of the velvet trimmed with gold, a view across the calm grey of the living room and the mock-Victorian clock-face. The sultry housewife awaiting her husband. Exactly my brand. But I can't take my own picture, can't even move, have to remain composed. Instead, I try to imagine Ted's reaction when he walks in. I'm realistic, I'm not expecting exultation or ecstasy; I'm only hoping for the warmth of familiarity, that maybe he'll say something like, "You clean up well," one of those backhanded compliments that I used to get at the beginning of our relationship, the ones that I clung to now as if they are little gems I can string into a necklace.

There was a time when I thought there might be a ring. In the very beginning, we'd talked about marriage. It was one of the first things his dad said to us when Ted introduced me: "There'll be wedding bells soon," he'd spluttered between gulps of beer and sloppy mouthfuls of Sunday roast. Wendy had smiled, genuinely, not yet believing I was there to stay. If I did it, I told them, even that early on because I knew where I stood, I would make it an intimate event. My friends all do these big, ostentatious weddings and they're so impersonal, don't you think? To which I received blank faces. Later Ted told me not to use words like "ostentatious", and not to talk about all the things I could afford that they couldn't, like I was rubbing it in their face. He wouldn't get angry, enjoyed it, even; drew sexual satisfaction from lecturing me on his cultural customs like I was some naughty schoolgirl. He saw me as a schoolgirl until he saw me as an old maid. Men aren't attuned to the nuances of age.

Maybe I was just too used to men telling me what to do. Dad was always scolding me, for everything. It was how he communicated. But especially for holding the gun wrong.

"Crouch, don't stand, girl! You need the stabiliser," he'd shout so loudly the birds would flutter away. "Tilt the barrel up. This isn't polo!"

I'd wonder in those moments why he was so adamant that I learnt to shoot. "This isn't a necessary life skill," I'd tell him. "I think I might be a vegetarian."

"Don't disappoint me twice in the same day," he'd bellow, before taking aim at another pigeon.

Then one day I got it right. I was fifteen. It was a dewy spring morning; fawns filled the fields and Dad told me he sensed that this was the season for me to redeem myself. Sizzling bacon at breakfast was followed by woolly socks in wellies and morning air still brisk from winter. I trudged down the muddy paths behind him, always five feet behind, making short sprints to keep pace with his bounding leaps. He was wearing the flat cap I hated. It made him generic, like he could have been any one of my friends' fathers roaming the fields for prey.

We reached the edge of the woodland. That was usually our destination – camouflage was key. We'd crouch down in one of the bushes and wait, sometimes hours, for a life to offer itself to us.

The taking of life had never bothered me. While the other girls at school protested on moral grounds to their fathers' cult-like obsession with hunting, Dad could sense that my pleas for precious little lives were disingenuous.

"You've never been a do-gooder," he'd tell me. "Don't change just because it's fashionable." That was Dad; morals were a fad, a plague of our time that would be cured when people were faced with the consequences of their petulant tantrums.

"People don't realise what it takes to uphold order, and they damn well don't appreciate the good it does them," he'd blurt out, his rifle flashing gloomy bronze in the pure white morning.

Later, Ted would tell me that only rich people felt entitled to take life for sport, told me only someone born into money would feel so comfortable playing God. It was the most poetic he'd ever been. For a moment, I felt sorry for him.

Dad was right: my qualms about our excursions centred not around their morality, but that they were boring.

"None of my friends have to do it," I'd try.

And he'd respond, "It's character building," and then shushing me as we skulked near the ground, the damp seeping under my skin. It would take the whole evening to warm up.

Often there'd be nothing, perhaps a partridge or a pheasant at most. (We'd carry the bird home and dump it on the kitchen counter. Then Mum would quietly instruct the maid to dispose of it. Outright rejecting Dad's offering was unthinkable.) Today, there was certainty in the air. The scene in front of us expectant, a picture anticipating its subject. Five minutes after we squatted down, a single deer hopped into frame. Dad's shrill eyes commanded me; my finger slid onto the trigger. The deer lifted its head and turned to face me, I was sure; it looked straight at me, its eyes alien and shiny black. Its hind legs twitched, but it didn't move. A gust of a sigh, then silence. Like it wanted me to kill it. I tilted the barrel of the gun up and closed one eye, like Dad always told me not to do. It didn't matter, though, I felt it; the script was already written. This was meant to be. I pushed through the mechanical resistance, then watched the deer fall before I heard the echo of the shot.

"Bull's eye," Dad said, and calmly lifted himself off the ground. I tiptoed behind him and glanced over his shoulder as he hunched down to inspect the beast. It lay there, serene. Its eyes as empty now as when it had been alive. I wondered if it was wrong that I saw no difference.

Dad carried it home over his shoulder, slowed down by its weight, so I could walk easily beside him. When we got home, we headed for the kitchen. He disappeared out the back door and returned half an hour later carrying skinless meat. He'd spared me the sight of carnage. He dropped the greasy hump on the kitchen table, and this time didn't abandon it to Mother or the maid.

"Get me a sharp knife," he ordered, and I turned to find the knife I'd seen the maid use on the birds. I handed it to him, watched him slice an incision, then put the knife down and split open the now formless meat. His fingernails bloodied as he peeled apart the mass, now just the memory of the animal we'd seen in the field. A kind of sourness I'd never smelt before; flesh at a standstill, stagnant moisture turning to slime. Dad's eyes remained steady and blue as they seared lines into the flesh for his hands and knife to follow. I watched him dissect the meat into chunks, laying them out like a disassembled puzzle. Some to be frozen, some eaten that day.

He washed his hands, and he turned from surgeon into chef. I'd never seen Dad cook before. I'd never seen him so full of love. His hands, still bloodstained, chopped and stirred and filled the room with sage and bay and rosemary and thyme. He made me chop onions and potatoes and I watched him arrange the meat on a baking tray, surrounding it with garlands of sweet marjoram and juniper berries. Mum entered the kitchen in the midst of our busy domestic bliss. I watched her face, its sullen bitterness, and I remember being smug; smug that I could prove to her that my father was a better man than she knew. That I'd brought that out in him.

Dad told me to invite a friend over for dinner, told me it was important to share the spoils of your achievements with the people you love. I called Jenny, who I knew despite her hippy tendencies still appreciated a good cut of venison. She came over, and Mum sat silently nibbling microscopic flakes of meat as the three of us gorged ourselves on rich, juicy chunks. Then we licked our fingers and spread ourselves by the fire, letting Mother and the maids clean up.

ELEVEN

I'm waiting for Ted to come home. I watch the hand sweep the clock-face, marking the passage of hours not minutes. I'm drowsy, my body still relaxed from my warm bath, my body melting into the soft fabric. Madness, I suddenly think, that I'd ever seen interior design as an alternative to personal grooming. The two complement each other so well. Fresh, clean body and space – together, they reflect a good soul. That's why interiors matter, isn't it? Even before the days of social media, your house was an advertisement; it showed the world the standard you set yourself. There was always a morality to it. Your body was part of that public face, had to be one with the showroom. A window display doesn't look the same with a scruffy homeless-looking person inhabiting it. Standards have to permeate your life like lavender in bath-room steam.

"Respect" was the word Ted used that day the chaise longue arrived. His proud mother, infuriatingly conceited, by his side.

"He knows what's best for him," she found it necessary to add.

Just you wait until they've left, I thought to myself. *See how brave you are then.*

Only, then, Ted surprised us all. He turned back, towards the hall, took the coat he'd just hung up back down from the coat rack and, without saying a word, walked out the front door.

The room fell silent.

"He's gone to the pub," Amy finally said, then looked at her mother for affirmation.

Like father, like son, I thought but didn't bother to say. Putting Wendy in her place seemed pointless now that Ted wasn't there to see it.

We stood there a while longer, unsure where this left us. It depended on how we interpreted his exit. If it was, as I suspected, a tantrum and he was to return to us that same evening, it was imperative that I stood my ground, making clear to Wendy that from now on Ted answered only to me. If, however, this was a bolder move, if this was Ted's way of saying he was done, then what Wendy thought was entirely inconsequential; she was out of my life. Her presence, in fact, could be entirely ignored. In either scenario, I decided, a tough front was a safe bet.

"It doesn't matter where he's gone, because he'll be back, and he'll be sorry." I glared at Wendy, silently adding, "And so will you."

Amy and Nancy seemed to be tired of the showdown. Amy had returned to her phone. Nancy was plucking at a loose thread on the fabric of the seat.

"Don't pull at that, it'll unravel," I snapped.

She looked up at me and sighed, then got up.

"Let's go, Mum." She plucked at Wendy's sleeve as she

walked to the door, not bothering to check if Wendy had followed her.

Wendy held my gaze for a few more moments, then turned and followed her daughter. Amy seemed to have vaguely noted the movement, got up from her seat, and walked to the door without looking up from her screen.

The door slammed.

"Good," I said, convincing myself that I'd won, although I knew that only Ted's next move could decide the victor.

Once again, I was waiting for Ted.

A baby, a girl, I think, sitting on a shelf, crying out for help. I wanted to cradle her in my arms, only when I approached, she broke open. I screamed in agony and looked down at the floor, expecting to find a broken skull, its contents splattered on the ground. Instead I found the baby had split open, revealing itself to be a Russian doll made of wood. It was a strange feeling, part relief, part sadness that the child I had mourned had never been real. Whatever it was, the feeling didn't last, because I was presented immediately with a facsimile of the original in which to vest my affection. I picked up the even smaller little girl, squeezing her chubby thighs to make sure that this one was definitely real. She squealed with joy, and I smiled down at her, convinced that I had found my calling in nursing the tiny thing. I offered her my pinkie as I rocked her. She sucked on it, drool running down my hand, dribbling down her cheek so that her head turned slimy and slipped from my grip. She fell to the floor. I looked down. Shards of wood lay at my feet. An even smaller fleshy thing crying out from amidst the rubble. I picked up the micro-

scopic baby – this was another girl, I sensed – and held her in my palm. I tried to make out the features of her tiny little face, tried to read the expression on her pinpoint of a mouth. I savoured the moment I had with her, but this time was wiser, already anticipated our inevitable parting. This would come to an end. Sadness in my heart, I lay the tiny princess on the ground, and walked away.

I woke up in a guilty sweat. I'd abandoned a baby. I'd left her there to die. I shouldn't have given up on her so prematurely. The helpless thing may have died in my palm, but there was no way of knowing. Who was I to anticipate the logic of that dream world? The only certainty was that without me she didn't stand a chance. Who had I become? Too weak to take a chance on anything, not even a hopeful young life. I pondered the dream, eyes wide open, staring ahead of me until the darkness turned to dawn, and the brightness, although it must have come gradually, suddenly shocked me awake.

I leapt out of bed. Something about waiting makes you unable to sit still. Your body mimes the movement you're missing. Perhaps it was also pride; I wouldn't have that wet blanket of a man derail me. I put on my kimono and made my way to the kitchen. Coffee would bring me back – to that wired state I was accustomed to, that I loved, that was better than feeling and sinking.

I filled the cup to the brim. When I looked at the shiny black stuff from a distance, let myself forget it was liquid water and bean, it looked lacquered, held that same otherworldly depth as a deer's eye. I stared into the cup, trying to summon my hunter's instinct. Only, the thought of the deer now evoked sweaty baby guilt, my head swerving on my neck like a limp puppet. I sat down at the kitchen table.

Ted was breaking me. I'd always been so resolute. For all the angst in my school days, the sadness of not belonging, I'd always had a plan, a clear direction, a way forward and out. I'd lost my inner compass; he'd broken it with his broken promises of a life he said he wanted and now didn't, a house that was a trojan horse containing emptiness. That's why I was swerving. It was all so terribly disorienting, navigating a void landscape of broken dreams.

I closed my eyes and the babies came back.

One, two, three. A gradient from biggest to smallest lined up in front of the wall, a shelf balancing on their heads, helping me find alignment. I walked up to them, tentatively. They seemed to have survived after all, but I didn't want to get my hopes up. I came closer still, then stumbled back as I felt, and smelt, the burning of the flesh of my chest. Red laser beams shot out from the babies' eyes. They were searing into me.

I snapped my eyes open and found that I was standing in front of the shelves I'd stacked next to the chaise longue a few weeks prior, in the hope that Ted would mount them to the wall. I seemed to have taken the matter into my own hands. I was holding a spirit level, the transparent bar filled with red liquid to indicate the straightness of the shelf's edge. Red like the babies' eyes.

Why were these demons haunting me? Babies, until now, had always been an abstract concept, the indiscriminate bundles in the prams of women I never talked to or wanted to know. Not at all the fragile realities occupying my dreams. Mum had never liked them, was very vocal about the fact that she wasn't "a baby person". She told me in her more affectionate moments as I was growing up that she liked me much better now, which, as far as I could see, still wasn't all that much.

Wendy was the first mother who talked to me about babies. I remember our first day together, just the two of us, with all the brain-blasting clarity of disinfectant scorching your airways. She'd come to help me unpack, had brought rubber gloves and a bucket full of cleaning products to help me "get the place in order". She'd rightly assumed I wouldn't know how to clean.

"Didn't teach ya that at home, did they?"

I couldn't tell if she was showing me out of kindness or to rub salt in the widening sore surrounding my inadequacy as a "missus". In the moment, though, I was grateful, accepted the pair of yellow gloves and followed her around the house as she sniffed and inspected like a fastidious mole. I watched in awe how she tackled even the most repulsive tasks without hesitation; her strong arms making mincemeat of murky brown coating the toilet bowl, obliterating patches of sticky grey I'd assumed were in the wall's colouring. When she started drilling hooks into the walls, I couldn't help but express my admiration.

"Doesn't Tony do the DIY?"

She scoffed. "Tony wouldn't know his arse from his elbow."

That was also the day I learnt where Ted got his expressiveness from.

"He's never lifted a finger. Even when I was pregnant with Ted, he didn't do nothing to help."

The acidity of the chemicals had made our noses run. I held my breath while she wiped her nose with her sleeve, then swung the hammer she was holding, expertly hitting the tiny hook resting between the fingers of her other hand straight into the wall.

"But you won't have to worry about that with my Teddy bear. I raised him right."

I remember the bash of the hammer accompanying the shock of the realisation that she simply assumed – didn't even bother to ask – that we were planning on having children. Like it could be no other way. As if there was some seamless connection between the hammering of the hook into the house we shared and the baby's head popping out from between my legs. I'd watched her then with her gaze fixed so resolutely ahead and knew that I was going to disappoint her.

The lasers scorched through me, still burning relentlessly red. My hands unclenched. The spirit level dropped to the floor. A metallic clang echoed until it merged with the jingling of keys in the lock.

TWELVE

I'm waiting for Ted to come home. I sink deeper into my chair, tinkering on the edge of consciousness. Only anticipation keeps me alert. Ted could walk in at any second. I have to greet him properly, or the whole thing will have been in vain.

My body is now perfect. Perfection defined not by contemporary beauty standards – a red herring, as Tina would have said, there to imprison women in a cycle of consumption of beauty products that didn't really help them where it mattered: at home. No, my body is perfect because it is clean, relaxed, cared-for. Because I am giving it the respect it deserves, on this love shrine dedicated to Ted. I close my eyes and zoom out of the picture, imagine it from the vantage point of an onlooker. I scan my body from head to toe with my mind's eye, a hyper-sensitive scanner now attuned to imperfections. It lands on my face. Of course, I'd been short-sighted once again. My picture isn't complete. Tina is always telling me about the importance of a polished finish, and I've completely neglected to colour my stripped-back facade. What I've created isn't the perfect picture, not even close; it is only a respectable canvas. What Ted wants, no, what he *needs*, is a finished painting. I anxiously eye the clock. He's already late; he could walk in the door any second. But this is a go-big-or-there-is-no-home situation.

I get up and run up the stairs, my breasts flapping as I skip several steps at a time. Once back in the bathroom, I grab my dusty makeup bag from the cupboard under the sink. Foundation. Primer. Blush. Bronzer. Highlighter. Eye pencil. Eye shadow. Mascara. Lipstick. Layer by layer, I am building the me that I need to be. That must be a slogan for a makeup brand I've heard somewhere. I brush and dollop and dab until there is not a single crack left on my immaculate surface. I am the perfect blend of accent, highlight and – essentially – camouflage. I put the bag back, tuck it behind the shampoos and lotions in the cupboard – part of my pristine perfection has to be its nonchalance. Ted can never see the behind-the-scenes. It has to be the perfect illusion. I cascade back down the stairs and reposition myself on my love-seat in my love dress. Now, I am truly ready.

If I'd thought that day about the picture Ted was walking into, of me in my kimono trying to hang up a shelf, perhaps I could have used that perspective to manage his emotions. Maybe I would have patted my hair flat, tried to adjust myself in some way so that I looked just a little less frazzled. Only, all this happened before I'd seen the light.

Ted walked into the room and sighed. I looked up at him from the metal bar that had landed just inches from my feet. *Just like the babies*, I thought.

Ted had timed his return well. He was, I was beginning to discover, a master at avoidance, knew how to make you wait so long your anger had dissipated by the time he got back. He had the patience for those tactics. And they say that women play games.

"You're home," I said, relieved despite myself.

"What're you doing now?" I froze at the exhaustion in his tone. Exhaustion that stung like the rejection I knew would follow.

"Just hanging these shelves up," I said, trying to sound perky.

Ted stood motionless for a few more moments. I silently recovered from the humiliation of being caught at the height of discombobulation. Eventually, I managed to drag my eyes up to look at him.

He looked tired. Bags under his eyes, but his beard casting that perfect five o'clock shadow, his hair charmingly ruffled. A pang of longing and regret – where had he been? I needed him back. I stared at him, helpless, not knowing how to ask him, not daring to face the truth of where he'd been.

Then, thank the relationship gods, he softened. He shook his head and walked over to me, picked up a shelf from the floor, and said, "Bring me a drill."

My man; my Ted.

I went to get the drill. It had been a while since I'd been in the garage. It had been a while since Ted had helped me with my DIY. It smelled especially musty: the deep, basal smell of a room shedding its skin. I inhaled deeply. Sometimes, people just need time. Especially men. That was something Tina could have said, probably would have reassured me, if I'd gone to see her after Ted had left.

I wondered if I'd made the right decision, storming out on her. I thought of her, sensed her presence through the garage walls, just a few yards away, really. I imagined her sitting there in the adjacent little box that made up the dimensions of her existence. It occurred to me suddenly that what I'd just endured was a perpetual condition for her. How excruciating it must be, waiting for a man you know you might never see again. How it must drain you, upholding the illusion she calls faith, that you would be reunited in the afterlife, convincing yourself every day that your life was purgatory, not hell.

I found the cardboard box labelled "Tools", one of the few boxes of Ted's possessions that we'd kept. There was another box, labelled "Ted's toys", containing his old Xbox, a drone and a child's "digger" his mum had given him.

"I used to love diggers," he'd told me the day we met his parents and his mum showed it to him, as if to remind him of his origins, a token of their undying bond.

"He used to love diggers," she'd repeated, smiling so maniacally I even then had to wonder if she was going to cause me problems.

Ted laughed when I'd shown him the box, humoured the reference to his slightly juvenile interests.

"Boy will be boys," he'd proclaimed and kissed me on the head.

When he'd asked me months later where his drone had gone, and I reminded him that it was with his other "toys", tucked away in the "garage, AKA the past, where it belonged", he seemed to have lost sight of the humour.

"I'm sorry I have hobbies that don't include furniture, or luncheons, or you," he'd snapped.

I'd made sure to return the drone to the box when he was done playing with it.

Ted needed his outbursts, small emancipations that let him feel like he wasn't losing himself. But he would always come around in the end.

I took the drill back to the living room. I handed it to him.

"You don't have to do this right now, you know. You can shower first," I said, knowing full well that he wouldn't risk putting it off and then having to deal with my "nagging" him later. I knew that instead he'd do it right now, and we'd do it – sweaty post-DIY sex, my favourite kind. I'd have Ted's glorious scent all over me once again.

"I'll get it over and done with," he mumbled, a screw already dangling from his lips while he adjusted the drill-head. I came up behind him, wrapped my arms around his thick torso, pushed my cheek against his neck. "Thanks for doing this," I smouldered, subtly sniffing for traces of women's perfume.

He remained stiff. "Do you want me to do this or not?" He shook me off and turned to the wall.

He hadn't quite forgiven me, that much was clear. He used to melt at the hint of my breath against his skin, turning him into a servile, love-devoted pup. What he was doing now, he was doing mechanically, out of duty. His soul had fled his body. A baby broke inside of me somewhere.

I watched him work, and when he was done I tried again; kissed him on his cheek to thank him, moved my hand down to his crotch. He pushed it away.

"Wait," he said. I stared at him, deflated. "I have something for you."

He disappeared into the hall. I listened to him fumbling with his coat and then stop in front of the door, as if gathering courage. He came back in holding a small box. *The* small box? Surely not? Ted wasn't the most emotionally adept, but surely he knew that this was not the time for a proposal. The mood was all wrong, and he wasn't a man for desperate gestures. He handed the box to me unceremoniously. "There you go," he said.

I held it in my palm. Red, velvet, a curly ribbon tied around it in a bow, compensating for the lack of wrapping, telling me it was a last-minute kind of gift, something he'd bought as an afterthought, or maybe in a rush. Out of guilt.

He hovered in front of me impatiently, his eyes darting to the stairs as if he had an urgent appointment to get to. I wanted to put him out of his misery, but I needed time to brace myself. If it was a ring, presented to me in the least romantic way imaginable, I had to decide what to do. Was this the time to grant him assurance? In the midst of a power struggle? One that it was essential I won if we were ever going to have a future? I twiddled the ribbon with my thumbs, watching the twirly ends bounce around all clown-like.

"Open it, then." Ted forced a quick smile.

I gave myself to my fate. I slid the pink band off and let it fall to the floor. Then I opened the box.

Small, subtle. No diamond. But it was a ring.

"You like it?"

"It's a ring," I said, taking it in, relief starting to replace any reservations I'd had. He wanted to be with me.

"You like it, then?"

I nodded and continued to stare at it. I felt him looking at me. Maybe he was trying to find the words, some kind of speech. Maybe he wanted to be the one to put it on my finger. I smiled and tilted the box towards him for him to take it out.

"Don't have to show it to me. I've seen it," he scoffed. "I wanted to get you something to make things alright. You girls like this kind of thing, don't ya?"

"So it's not–" I snapped the box shut and looked him straight in the eyes. "Yep," I said, was all I could muster while stifling my mortification.

"Good." He turned away, satisfied that he'd done his duty.

I watched him; I couldn't move. I was paralysed, confounded by the possibility that two people could occupy such wholly different realities.

"I'll take that shower now." Ted disappeared up the stairs.

I stayed standing there with the box in my hand, rubbing my thumbs across the prickly velvet.

THIRTEEN

I'm waiting for Ted to come home. The light outside dims, which irritates me because with all the makeup I'm wearing, for once, I would have looked good even in the direct sun. I suddenly realise that, now that it is getting darker, the nudes and browns I've selected for my eyes and lips won't be as striking. Night-time is for smoky eyes and red lips. A chill passes over me. My body, by now, has cooled off completely from my steaming. A quick dash up the stairs will get my blood flowing. I get up and head for the bathroom. Once there, I dig up the dusty makeup bag again, extract the – even dustier – "going-out" makeup, and apply it to my face like thick cement. My skin, by now, is dry and taut. I try to relax the muscles in my face to stop my paint job from cracking.

Ted always liked heavy makeup on me. I used to cake it on in the early days like his love for me depended on it. Like the compliment was actually a precondition. It was unnatural, out of character, I told him. But I did it anyway. I think I did it as a kind of apology. Like at some level I knew that I'd consumed him with my vision. I was the room he lived in, the walls he looked at every day; he was allowed to enjoy a change of interior. So I did it, showing up at the pub on Fridays, looking increasingly like his friends – glowing gold with foundation in the night, drunkenly scrubbing at my face before I went to bed. I didn't want to stain the sheets. Then he'd complain because he wanted to "fuck me all dolled-up". I told him he couldn't have his cake and eat it. The thing is, he never cared about having the cake as much as I wanted to believe. He just wanted to guzzle it all up. While I baked and polished and preserved, he wanted to sink his teeth into bite after delicious bite with no regard for the consequences.

A flutter of anger passes through me, threatening to make me abandon my blusher brush. So I conjure Mum. Telling me to keep my eyeshadow subtle, to stick to nudes, ladylike. Numb. To fade into pasty English rose, into dewy and passionless and bland. That reanimates me. I pick up my darkest eyeliner and extend the already thick lines into cat eyes. Then, I return to my love seat, my insides brewing with plosive powder and itchy scrawls caked in sticky muck.

The sound of running water. Ted was actually taking a shower, not only trying to avoid my touch. Washing away his sins. Who knew? Maybe I'd gone too far. He felt hard done by – the poor thing – probably used. I didn't want to admit it, but I was conjuring Tina, imagining what she'd say.

"Do something for him, something that makes him feel special. Something that has nothing to do with your Instagram or your furniture." These were the words of a relationship veteran.

And so, I took him to the only place I knew to connect with a man.

"Was hoping for a quiet one," he complained as I ushered him into the car the following morning. "Please, no outlets today."

I smirked. "We're not going to the outlets."

Ted didn't like surprises. They made him nervous, he said. I always thought that spoke to the lack of trust he had in me. I glanced at him as I drove. He was twiddling his thumbs like he was worried I was driving him to a cliff edge to push him over.

We drove the next hour in silence. Ted didn't utter so much as a grunt until I pulled up to the family home.

"You taking me to Mum and Dad for a scolding?" he half-joked, obviously nervous. I said nothing. It wasn't a bad idea. "Could have warned me. I didn't wear my Sunday best."

I shrugged off the insecure banter. I was bored of it.

"We're not going in to see them. Relax." I stopped the car and got out, then opened the boot and pulled out my wellies.

"You could of warned me," he grumbled as he watched me wriggle my feet into the boots. I ignored him.

"Here." I handed him his trainers; he didn't have any boots. "It'll get muddy."

He pulled an expression that was sceptically curious. The same face he used to pull when he'd visit my home in the early days, or when I'd say something so shamefully upper-class that he couldn't contain himself. I'd missed that face tinted with affection.

"Let's go." And I turned, marching ahead of him towards a stile leading into the fields. He hesitated, then finally took a run-up before dramatically throwing himself over the fence like a schoolboy in need of attention. I walked on ahead of him, always five yards ahead, just like Dad. He trailed along behind me, kicking at rocks and picking up sticks along the way. When we reached the forest edge, I stopped and scoured the area for good cover. My eyes fell on a bush I was sure was the same one Dad had chosen that day of the deer.

"Come," I ordered Ted, then crouched down among the crunchy leaves.

He frowned at me, bemused. "You gonna bury me alive?" There it was: Ted's deepest fear predictably disguised as cheeky banter.

"Just do it, Ted."

The soil beneath the crunch was moist, warmer than that day in early spring with Dad. I hadn't considered that perhaps autumn wasn't the time for conjuring life. But it didn't matter, I told myself, it was the principle.

I crouched down lower to the ground and pulled at Ted's collar to join me.

He looked at me.

"You've actually lost it, haven't you?"

"You said to me once, when I told you about hunting, that you thought it was growing up the way I did that made me happy to take a life."

"I'm not killing nothink." He crossed his arms like a stroppy child. I could almost see the snot running from little Teddy bear's nose.

"Relax, Ted, I'm unarmed. I just want to show you what it's like."

"What, we pullin' the legs out of ants?"

Let it go. Be generous, said a voice in my head I couldn't admit was Tina's.

"Quite the opposite, actually," I said. "Just wait."

We lay side by side, Ted shuffling, me shushing him, both of us looking out across the small clearing ahead. We waited a good two hours before there was rustling.

"What is it?" Ted's voice cascaded across the clearing, the birds scattering up from the canopies.

"Brilliant," I sighed and sat up. "You scared it off."

"Who cares? There's no point anyway."

"There might be. Now you won't find out."

"It's always just a power trip with you."

I soaked up his malice but said nothing. Like a good girl-friend.

"Can you just try to trust me?" I finally said, sharper than I'd hoped.

Ted scoffed, but lowered himself back to the ground.

We waited another hour, maybe two. I felt my body sinking into the rich ground, swaddled by its fertile wetness, lulling me into a comforting sleep. I was on the brink of consciousness when the shape of a chestnut mare appeared in the clearing.

Ted shook me but thought better than to speak this time, aware of how close we were to its powerful hooves. We watched the impressive animal graze on the few remaining leaves, her colour so perfect against the autumn palette. She edged towards us as she ate her way through the bushes at a leisurely pace. Ted twitched.

"Let's go."

"We can't, it'll spook her," I whispered back.

She jerked, raised her head. I felt Ted's body brace itself to get up.

"Stay down."

"It'll trample us," he whined but stayed put.

The mare sniffed around, moving in closer still, hooves pressing into the ground next to our faces. I clenched my jaw and closed my eyes, surrendering.

Crunching, panting, pause. Retreat. I listened to the receding steps for a while, then opened my eyes.

Ted's head was still plastered to the ground.

"She's gone."

Ted tilted his face towards me, looking at me, grateful. Like I was the one who had just chosen to spare his life.

"Such a movie moment." I grinned. "Close brush with death bringing the lovers closer." I let it go unsaid that he'd absolutely failed me as a hero. That much we already knew.

"Jesus Christ, Rosie."

"I know. Exciting, isn't it?"

I watched him open his mouth to argue, then reconsider, collapsing back down into the bed of damp. I'd placated him at last.

I gave him a few minutes to recuperate, then got up, brushing the sticky mud from my waxed Barbour coat. I reached out a hand. "We can go now."

Ted raised himself stiffly onto his knees, then took my hand and stood up. We started the walk back to the car.

He walked closely beside me. I flinched when he grabbed my hand, but then let him squeeze his sweaty fingers into my cool palms.

"Did you know that horse?" he eventually asked.

"I didn't even realise we had horses. Probably one of the neighbours'. Maybe it escaped."

"So what did you think it was?"

Impending doom. That was something I could never explain to him.

He shrugged. "It's like I always said: you posh people will be the death of each other."

I doubted that was something Ted had ever said. "Is that what you want?"

He shook his head. "No." He sounded defeated.

"I just wanted you to see that hunting, it's not killing things.

Sometimes it means you have to risk your life to take it. You surrender yourself to nature, and sometimes you're lucky, but not always. And you come out with respect for life. We take responsibility for the trigger we pull anyway every time we buy a cut of lamb. And when you eat an animal you hunted, you really savour it. It's humbling, that's what Dad always said." I hoped I hadn't undermined myself by quoting my daddy. I could still smooth it over with something profound. "Everyone is so fixated on the kill, but that's not the climax, that comes before, when you face the threat of your own extinction. That's what life is all about."

"For the poor little bugger, dying's a bit of a turning point." He forced a half grin. It wasn't that he didn't understand me, I knew that now. It was that he was afraid of losing himself once he admitted he did. He held my hand all the way back to the car.

FOURTEEN

I'm waiting for Ted to come home. I wait. I wait until the pitch-black night has cloaked my meticulous masterpiece entirely. Ted won't see a thing. He'll leave the lights off when he finally gets home, sneak in like he usually does, and will probably walk right by me. If he does decide to switch the light on, though, I realise, he'll see my heavily made-up face in the bright artificial light, and it will look more ghoulish than demure.

Maybe I was my mother's daughter after all. I want it to look like I am trying hard for the relationship, not to be beautiful. There's nothing more unattractive than a woman trying too hard. That was the one thing both my parents would always agree on. Although with them it was hard to tell if they'd tried at all. It was hard to imagine what trying between them would have looked like. It was enough to make you severely uncomfortable. They were proud, so stubbornly defensive it was like they were trying to protect something, themselves, probably, from each other. So dysfunctional, I used to think.

I get up and stumble to the bathroom, remove the red lips with a wet wipe, replace it with a lighter tint, the eyelids back to brown. I touch up the highlights for good measure. I look at my shadowy face in the mirror. Dark circles under my eyes somehow looking puffy and sunken at the same time. Like me. How could a person be simultaneously so bloated with the fight, so proud and defiant, and yet agonisingly fragile, excruciatingly empty? I want to understand it, to wrap my mind physically around these contradictions splitting me in parts, to swaddle them into the wholeness I'd lost. I want to blame my parents, or Ted, or myself. I want one enemy – one problem. I want to fix whatever it is and my own brokenness. But any attempt makes me light-headed, pulling me into a nauseating tornado of cosmic colours, all constellations knotted with wormholes, shaking up my sense of reality like metallic stardust trapped inside a sand-timer. Easier to fix my face, now incredibly itchy. I refrain from scratching, resolutely adding more foundation under the eyes.

The sun had already set by the time we arrived from our faux hunt. There was a peace between us, the kind of peace that comes with early autumn dusk.

I turned on the kitchen light. The house glowed yellow. I put the kettle on. Ted went upstairs to shower, this time, I trusted, only to warm up. I poured hot water into a pot and put it on the familiar tray along with the biscuits I knew he liked – hobnobs, bland with a bit of crunch. Very fitting.

The whole experience has been so immersive, I hadn't checked my phone once, and was only tempted to take a snap when I looked down at the teapot on its tray, the image of a domestic autumn night. I resisted. Today, I would be present for Ted.

When I heard him at the stop of the stairs, I carried the display to the chaise longue. He appeared in the doorway in his dressing gown and slippers, a soft smile on his thin lips that dropped the second he saw where I was sitting.

"Can we do this on the sofa?"

I waited for the punch line, but it didn't come.

"You're serious?" I said.

His expression remained flat. "I can't relax and drink my tea on that thing."

"It's just a chair, Ted, no need to get all emotional about it."

"You get emotional about the furniture all the time."

I frowned. "I thought we'd made up."

"What, because you took me on some ego – oh whoops, I mean, hunting trip?"

"I was trying to fix things."

"Things will be better when you return that bloody chair like I asked."

"It's just a chair!"

"I told you, Rosie, it's not about the chair. It's about respect, alright? You show me some, and we can move forward. Until then, I'm out."

He got up and turned to storm out the front door, then realised he was wearing his dressing gown, which was laughable. It derailed him only momentarily before he turned and went upstairs instead. I left him to his tantrum. I couldn't tell him what he wanted to hear; I wasn't going to get rid of the chair, because it was ridiculous.

Instead, I sat seething from my spot in the living room until I was too tired to be angry. Only then did I make my way upstairs and lie myself next to the slumbering oaf, agitated again as I watched him sleep like a baby in the midst of our crisis. I glared at him into the dawn, growing steadily delirious. As the sun began to rise, the silhouette of his mound beneath the sheets began to resemble the chaise longue.

I was back in the room with the chaise longue. I approached her, trailed my fingers along her curved edge, appreciating her. She was a woman; I was sure of it. The intensity of my affection for her surprised me. She was something between child and mother, past and future, or maybe both. Whatever she was, she was part of me, and I knew that as long as I could hold onto her, I'd survive. I wanted to hug her. I ran up to her like she was a long-awaited lover and wrapped my arms around one of her legs, clutching onto her silky wood. Suddenly, the ground beneath me started to crumble, the smooth tiles breaking into bricks like Tetris blocks. Desperately, I tried to pull myself up onto the chair. I sat on it and looked down into the darkness, the chair now a floating island in empty space. For a moment, I felt safe, until three pairs of laser-beam eyes appeared from behind the far end of the chair. The babies crawled up onto the seat and turned their gazes to the cushioning that held me, then fell to their hands and knees and dug their fang-like teeth into the padding, biting out huge chunks like ravaged lions, tossing them aside into the great beyond. The seat disappeared from under me as the babies advanced. Closer, closer. I screamed into the void.

I woke up. He wasn't there to save me. The mound that was Ted had disappeared. I threw the covers off and made my way downstairs. Checking frantically behind furniture, I still hoped that it was all just a game of hide-and-seek. But our game wasn't trivial anymore, and Ted had run again.

FIFTEEN

I'm waiting for Ted to come home. Now that I've optimised my face for the evening lighting, I can rest easy. I collapse back onto my seat and watch the door, wide-eyed. I try not to think about what is keeping him. The already implausible work excuse no longer holds up. It is quarter past eleven, the clock on the wall tells me. By now the thought of him with another woman incites not anger, but fear. I can't explain why, but it is as if a damp patch starting in my chest is spreading across my entire body and, without him, I will disintegrate like wet wallpaper. Goosebumps spread across my skin, but I refrain from hugging my arms around my body, just in case Ted walks in at that precise moment and sees the image of a feeble foetus, rather than the seductress I want to be.

The cold is hard to bear, but even more excruciating is resisting the burgeoning urge to document the process. The vibrant light of a photo on my screen would warm my soul, I know, would help me last the wait; in fact, it would make the wait more meaningful. The absolute seismic, life-changing awesomeness of Instagram lies in its ability to make every moment of a mundane human life matter. Sitting on the sofa can be transformed into a performance, a piece of art; it can reach someone and inspire them. Instagram is a solace: no matter how long you wait, a picture makes wasted time valuable.

But that also means that taking a picture is giving up. My repeat offence betrays my lack of faith, shows that I don't trust Ted is coming back: a picture is a consolation prize, personal insurance; is pre-emptively accepting defeat. I have to commit myself to selflessness. I have to hope. And when you risk everything, you have no choice but to hope.

Ted did come back after he ran the second time. But never fully. Only intermittently. He treated the pristine home I'd made like a shoddy motel you resort to for a few hours' kip. He didn't talk to me, grunted, perhaps; told me he was tired when I asked him how his day was, what he'd been doing, whether he still liked me at all.

I spent my time walking through the ominous void he left – a dark wood full of wiry branches and hidden traps. A tap that dripped every time I turned to walk away, then stopped when I turned back; a lightbulb that flickered at the precise moment a wave of panic passed over me; the crumbling edges of plaster along the ceiling, taunting me with the possibility of collapse.

Sometimes, I thought this place resembled the woodland at home. It seemed familiar. Only, the soil that had held me that day we'd waited for the horse was now full of worms. And when I sat still too long, they would begin to eat into me like I was already dead.

Other times, it reminded me of my own bush. It had the same dark, wiry beauty about it – both ominous and intoxicating. It had given me great pleasure, growing it out over the years that Ted was losing interest in me sexually. It was empowering, allowing myself to get lost in a world he couldn't access to appreciate. Perhaps if you'd asked Ted for the moment our relationship began to go definitively south, he would have pointed correspondingly downwards, to my nether regions; perhaps, to the moment my frizzy pubes begun to protrude from my increasingly decent underwear. I assumed he wouldn't like it – the abundant growth – although I'd never asked. If his taste in women was anything to go by, I always thought, trimmed and contained were his style. That's what he thought I was – "proper". Choosing someone who grew up on tweed and repression was surely a safe bet, he'd thought, for the kind of unproblematic femininity he wanted. A clean, quiet girl who kept her emotions and her pubic hair in check. No matter how animalistic our sex, I knew that was what he really wanted. Too bad. He should have tended to his garden. Now I was taking it back.

It was easy to let the eternal twilight of the wood lull you to sleep. Only the flashy lights of Instagram kept me alert. It was comforting to see that the worse I felt, the shinier my facade. I dug through my archive of pictures, the ones attesting to our domestic bliss. Me with Ted at dinner; me with Ted, both of us wearing red, standing in front of coordinated potpourri in shades of purple; me with Ted and a freshly baked Bundt cake, his arms wrapped around me, and our faces so alive you wouldn't for a moment doubt that our love had a pulse. I posted them all. I posted them with the most uplifting, euphoric quotes I could find. "Home is where your heart is", a timeless classic for the classic dinner pic. "Home is not a place, it's a feeling" for the passionate popery. For the pièce de resistance, the picture of the lovers entangled beside the Bundt: "Home. Where love and dreams join. Where today and tomorrow become forever."

Whatever happened, at least nobody would get the satisfaction of watching me fall. Jenny would never know. The girls from school would never know. None of them would see behind the curtain. If I was going to have my domestic dream brutally butchered, at least the fantasy would live on; at least there'd be a virtual dimension where I'd proved to all the disbelievers that I was victorious.

I spent the rest of the evening drinking tea to avoid eating chocolate, and intermittently checking the status of my likes on the three photos. The numbers ascended steadily. The dinner picture did the best – the least innovative pictures always did. Instagram needed time to catch up to creativity. But the risqué ones sizzled, slowly over time, slowly rousing people to your vision. You just had to keep pushing, building your following, until the sheer mass of their conglomerated thumbs over your pictures pulled them to your mighty centre of gravity. People always came around in the end.

The likes helped, but I needed more than mindless mass approval. I needed to talk. It was as though Jenny sensed that, her radar impeccably attuned to desperation. It was during those long, lonely evenings in the cold, dark wood that Jenny forced her way back into my life, squeezed her fat posterior through a crack I'd left her – a door slightly ajar was all it took. I knew that. I had to be honest: she didn't come totally uninvited. I left the door ajar, I offered the ambivalent yes–maybe invitation, coy like a 1950s housewife.

It started at night. In bed. Me next to the already snoring Ted, or sometimes next to the dent in the pillow where his head should have been, and was increasingly not. Jenny started messaging me from another bed, a four-poster in a much bigger, perhaps even more isolated, mansion somewhere. She was lying next to "some old man". She never specified who, always made a point of shrouding him in anonymity; a clear message: she was uninhibited and unattached. Free. So untethered compared to me, the housewife who had chosen boredom and shackles over a friendship with her. I let her punish me, let the insinuations glide over me like a silk nightdress; in the empty bed of my dollhouse, they felt like affectionate teasing, the juvenile jibes of a boy at school who likes you.

At first, it felt adulterous. Like each slide into a DM was an intimate betrayal of my new life with Ted, me toying, however tentatively, with the possibility of returning to an intoxicating simplicity. The safety of friendships openly built on mutual dissatisfaction. One in which our future could only ever be a crumbling vestige of the present. Safety, not through fortification inside a domestic dream, but from the assurance that comes with expectations as low as the ruins of the walls around you.

One night, she told me about her man's penis. "I'm not sure if it classifies as a micro-penis, but it's small, trust me." In this case, I did – trust her, believe her. On the sordid details of her imperfect life, she was always brutally honest. "It's like I have to compromise on everything, you know? He doesn't even like yoga."

Compromise. For a moment I wondered why she was with him if that's how it felt. Ted always liked to tell me about "opportunity cost". He liked to talk about economics, about concepts in finance that he'd picked up from work, things I knew nothing about; nobody with money ever did, he said. People make rational decisions, he'd tell me. They weighed up the cost of their choice in terms of the next best alternative they'd forego, what they'd have to give up. That's what he did, he said. Every choice he made was measured, he'd say, and so, rest assured, that when he chose me, it was carefully considered, he knew what it meant, he was completely certain. It wasn't romantic, but, in the moment, the certainty was tantalising. Certainty always is. But the concept of opportunity cost, it seemed, applied to the decisions of men in skyscrapers, looming high above the houses of the festering chaos of human life. Down here, costs weren't calculated, only became apparent over the course of time. Compromise revealed itself after promises were made and broken, your choices never a clean, transactional event, but a stochastic hiccup; the extended flatulence that follows the meal we thought would complete us as it is slowly broken down. Just like Jenny, I was compromising too.

"Why don't we just run away together?" Jenny went on to ask me. "Like the time in the Lake District," she said, evoking a trip that had become the trip that broke us. A trip that had been a retreat. "We'd do it properly this time," she said, not leaving time for the memory to descend and squash the optimism of her plans. "Only this time it would be in the open, actually moving in. Instead of boys who come and go, we'd be choosing to stick together, we'd support each other without all the drama. Living our best life."

The familiar vacuousness of her one-liners made me smirk in the dark. "Sounds a bit co-dependent, don't you think?" I blinked, the glow of my phone now starting to dry out my eyes. "We'd hold each other back. We always did at school. Just look at how much more we've done since we left."

I watched the pulsating ellipses on the screen, churning along with Jenny's brain as she conjured up a way to convince me I was wrong. "It's funny," she finally replied, "that what in a friendship people say is co-dependent, in a romantic relationship is called love."

I turned off my screen light, put the phone, facing down, on my white-wood, charming cottage-romance bedside table.

Even with the light off, her words pulsated through my head like her insidious ellipses. I gave in to the thought. I imagined us in a house together, maybe an apartment, somewhere in a city, because this would be a modern arrangement. I imagined how we'd take it in turns to cook, how she'd value our catch-up over dinner as much, perhaps even more, than I did. If I could find a way to live for Jenny, I thought, I would be free. I would be living in a house with an open ceiling. I would look up and, instead of the white-grey descending over me, I would see only sky. Fresh, brisk air and the kind of light that sprinkles you with dew.

Wearing a turtleneck without wondering if Ted would miss my cleavage. Breathing deep. Every day I would breathe, would want to look around and see what I found, open to the possibility, no need to curate my showroom, no need to control – because I wouldn't be afraid of what I'd find. There would be no secrets in this house, no need, no roof to come tumbling down. Nothing at stake, only conversations in the light.

SIXTEEN

I'm waiting for Ted to come home. Eleven thirty-five, the clock tells me, not that it really means anything to me now. Time is no longer linear. Less a force propelling me forward, more a tangled knot of weeds pulling me into a swamp, deeper and deeper into an underworld I am sure is what therapists mean when they use the term "subconscious". I move through the disorientating space, by now also painfully familiar, searching for something to latch onto, anything to steady me. I find a clump of mud and reach for it. If I stay still long enough and cling to it, I tell myself, the world will eventually stop spinning. The branches won't lurch for me like ominous tendrils. The water will release me from its tar. If I hold on tight enough, I won't feel quite so trapped by the scary wood. I dig my finger-tips deep into the sticky mud.

Not long after we'd begun our late-night affair, Jenny posted a story announcing that her father had died. The announcement was just one, unassuming picture in her story – his face super-imposed over a wilting flower. "I'll miss you, Dad. May your spirit live on in the vibrations we call love." This was followed by a string of shots of various rooms of the family home – now hers, I guessed – and a request for her followers to rate the best yoga spots. An hour later, she'd triumphantly announced that the orangery was contest winner.

And then came the day's big reveal. Jenny defied individualistic notions like birth and death. We were just specks in the universe: how could anyone's death possibly be at the centre of the day's news? Far more important was that she would be repurposing the orangery of her childhood home to start a yoga studio. It was all rather despicable, but the one thing you could trust Jenny to do was give you permission. I could message her my condolences while I still hated her, and it would be nothing compared to her overt amorality. My fingers hovered over the keys as I tried to decide between condolences and congratulations. I settled for connection:

I remember bunking off French class to get high in that orangery.

She read my message immediately, then made me wait two hours before a message appeared on my screen:

My father dies and that's what you send me?

Typical Jenny. Testing people even across cyberspace. I'd never understood what she wanted from me. Especially not since school, after she'd "found herself". My "materialistic way of life" disgusted her, she made that clear (ironic, of course, given that she had stayed living off Daddy's money to pursue a life detached from the frivolous human needs for food, clothing and shelter). But even the enlightened Jenny had struggled to let go. She'd latched on, called me every night for a good six months after I moved away. Every call was the same. After the initial outburst berating me for my capitalistic nightmare of a life, she'd proceed to bombard me with new concepts that she called "Buddhism", although I was pretty sure most of the one-liners were direct quotes from the Instagrams of LA "yogis", AKA women who pranced around in spandex pretending that it was their mantras not their mammary glands that were attracting a following. I'd listen to her, never hung up on her. I endured the first two movements of her symphony because I knew that the final half was always more honest. That's when she'd show me her vulnerable side, telling me about her dating life, or something about how trapped she was feeling in her house, or how she missed me. Sometimes she'd even ask me how I was. And then I'd start to think that she needed me as much as she needed yoga not to feel like a failure.

Then, one day, the phone calls stopped. A good sign, I thought. She didn't need me anymore. Me: sane, steady, guardian to her lost soul, the one always less susceptible to fads that demanded reinvention. If she'd finally flown the nest, I was happy for her. We'd finally moved on. I was used to being the bigger person.

So sorry to hear about your dad.

I hesitated.

Should I come to the funeral?

Two days later she answered me.

It was today. Soz.

To Jenny, everything was leverage. Events like death, morally cordoned off for most mortals, weren't off limits to her. Our conversations in the cold of the night had started to melt me, but I remembered now that it hadn't just been my family that had made me want to leave my childhood home. It was her too. Her with her nonsense that sucked you in and churned you up. Being friends with her was losing yourself. She was so adept at coaxing, it always surprised me that she hadn't managed to find an obliging boyfriend to pander to her. Perhaps that wasn't enough of a challenge.

Be the bigger person.

Dinner at my parents' tomorrow? Like old times?

I pressed send and immediately cringed at the faux pas. "Parents". *Eek.* I waited a day, monitoring her Insta-activity closely, the stream of meaningless mantras and foliage, irritated but also a little hopeful when she posted a generic photo of a river with a quote by her yogi "Christine" about "forgiving quickly". She replied straight afterwards:

Fine.

Jenny's way of saying she'd love to, that she needed me more than ever. I breathed deep as I felt my spirit cross the threshold of my familiar walls – a trip out and about, under the clear, open sky.

*

"Christine says buy a plant and water it." Jenny led me into the orangery. "So, I went all-out and got really tropical. Most of them were likely indigenous to India, so, you know, I'm connected spiritually, through their roots." She looked at me, deadly serious.

I looked around the room packed so full of ferns and citrus fruits that the architecture of the Edwardian greenhouse was completely lost. But I couldn't expect Jenny to understand the nuances of interior design – that it was all about accentuating a room's features.

"I made you a pie," was all I could think to say in response, handing her a blackberry and apple tart. "Picked the berries and everything."

"I'm sure you did. Mrs Nigella Lawson reincarnate over here," She was using that bitchy voice she'd learnt at school, the one she was never cool or pretty enough to pull off.

She put the pie dismissively on an art deco side table. A good choice, I had to admit. I followed her deeper into the foliage until we reached a yoga mat surrounded by candles.

"This is the epicentre, like the room's chakra. I calculated it and everything."

She was testing me, I knew. My scepticism only ever intensified the stream of airy-fairy word vomit. She glared at me, challenging me to be dismissive.

I searched for the words to keep the peace. "It's a great backdrop. You'll get some great shots in here."

She raised an eyebrow at me. "Because you're the expert on all things interior design now too, right?"

I wasn't sure what to say. *As much as you're the next Mahatma Gandhi,* was what came to mind, but then I looked around the room teeming with green life, manically compensating for the one she'd just lost, and I stopped myself. "We should get going. Told Dad we'd be there at seven."

She perked up at the opportunity to derail my plans. "Just one tea in here. I want to christen it. Christine says to make tea and drink it."

I stared at her, already exhausted.

"Your dad will understand. Trust me, he gets these things."

I tried for a moment to conjure a world in which Jenny knew my father better than I did, one in which he was in any way sympathetic towards the teachings of an online yogi – a woman of all things – but it hurt my head. Much easier to dismiss this as another one of Jenny's convenient truths.

"Well, if Christine says so." I smirked but Jenny wasn't amused. She turned solemnly to a bamboo platform she'd set up next to the yoga mat and began pouring the tea. We sat down and sipped it from miniscule cups.

Jenny smiled at me, eyes rolling loose in their sockets, lacking focus. She looked deranged. "So glad we're reconnecting in this way. I always knew you'd come around. Saw it with my third eye."

I sipped my tea silently, pretending to look around the room.

"We should practise together sometime. Think it could really help you work through some of that pent-up tension." She left it hanging in the room: the suggestion that I needed help. Like I'd ever need her help.

"I'm not that stressed," I said curtly.

"We're all stressed." She drained her cup of tea and stared at me. "How're things with Ted?"

"Fine," I said, a bit too stiffly.

"Must be hard, trying to breach that void."

I'd kept Jenny away from Ted. She was there the day we met. Almost sabotaged me, of course. I was selling scones at the village fete, a humiliating tradition for the women of the estate that Mum made me uphold. Ted was there with his football team – they'd been playing in the fields outside the village and had stumbled across the fete in search of a pub. He'd spotted me from "a mile away", he told me later; he decided to buy a scone even though he'd "never had one in his life". Jenny had loomed over us, making snide remarks about him and his "chimp" friends, about football being the Primark of sports, about how it reduced people to "tribal hooliganism" and said a lot about a person if they liked it, even more than the fact that they'd never had a scone. Ted had pulled a face – admittedly chimp-like. But I'd ignored it, and I'd ignored her. I'd apologetically handed him a scone – "in exchange for a pint," I told him.

Looking at her now, I was more certain than ever that I'd made the right decision. Even if Ted did leave me, I'd escaped her.

She waited to see if her trap would catch. When she realised I wasn't going to take the bait, she got bored, crawled onto her front and poked her bum in the air for a downward-facing-dog.

"We really should get going, Jen."

"You need to tune in to the pace of the universe."

I winced.

When we were eighteen, we'd rented a house together. It was the end of secondary school and everyone else had gone on graduation trips to Southeast Asia or Costa Rica or Japan in groups of ten or fifteen. We only had each other. Far-off places didn't appeal to us, maybe because we were scared; maybe because we didn't think the two of us could live up to the social media-worthy hype such a trip was expected to generate. Instead, we chose a rustic cottage in the Lake District. Instead of finding ourselves, we'd centre ourselves, Jenny said, while I just felt obliged to do something, anything at all to keep Mum off my case. Sitting at home, of course, was "unsociable", a crime worthy of a thorough shunning in her books. So we went, the two of us, to our mountain retreat, to go and be hermits of the socially acceptable kind.

Jenny had just discovered "Yoga with Christine": "the people's yogi," she kept repeating, as if that made her some kind of Good Samaritan too. Truth was, Jenny had opted for yoga because she wasn't pretty enough to pull off bulimia. While the other girls at school channelled Blair Waldorf in *Gossip Girl* with their wiry legs and heavy eye makeup to hide the deepening semi-circles under their bulging eyeballs, Jenny knew that she couldn't afford to look tired. She had the kind of face that needed all the help it could get. So, she'd made the aesthetically informed life-choice of doing yoga six times a day instead. People might never envy her for her looks, but she was going to make damn sure that her Zen was a coveted commodity.

And now she had the medium to make her point. Instagram had just launched, and Jenny was going to harness its powers to show everyone how brightly her light shone. The proof was in the followers.

We spent the weeks floating through the mountains like two roaming souls. At the crack of dawn, the clear air and endless fields lured us out. We'd walk, with only Google Maps and an unreliable connection to guide us. It didn't matter, though; we sensed where we should go, always miraculously hit a road in the end, and always eventually found a taxi or a bus to take us home. Jenny was enthralled with the picturesque backdrop, her business acumen piqued.

"I literally couldn't have planned it better. I mean, this is like Buddha meets fucking Wordsworth. So Romantic with a capital 'R': totally my brand. Heritage meets Zen. East meets West."

"Nope, that's colonialism," I'd told her sarcastically, but it didn't register. She was already lost to her mission of ever-so-eclectic cultural appropriation. The kind of thing I knew any university student was going to hate her for. But it was unlikely she'd end up going to uni.

"I can learn everything I need to from ancient religious texts," she'd told me. And in her case, she was right; there wasn't any practical need for her to go to university. Her parents were much more amenable to sustaining her life of privilege than Dad with his bizarre notions of getting a job for "character building". She'd be free to follow her moronic impulses until she self-destructed. I knew that one day she would.

We walked tirelessly, only stopping when Jenny forced us to. Then she'd strike a yoga pose and make me take a picture. Her in lotus pose beside a tree. Her in downward-facing-dog against the swirling mountain skies. I obeyed begrudgingly, resisting the urge to push her, as she squatted in "low lunge" at an especially jagged cliff edge.

In the evenings, we cosied up in our lodge by the fire and worked our way through the supply of chocolate-covered Digestives that to Jenny were the height of indulgence and to me were stodgy and bland. I munched on the second-rate treats while she intermittently made her selection of pictures for her Instagram and compared them to those of the popular girls on their exotic adventures.

"I swear to god, they're actually getting thinner."

I watched her eyes scan their waistlines, measuring them against her own in a photo of her silhouette as thick as the tree beside her.

"They probably have Delhi-belly," I offered while I stared into the fireplace, transfixed by the flames.

"I wish I could make food poisoning look hot." She stared into her screen until I thought it would shatter, then finally threw her phone down on the plush rug beneath us.

We stared into the flames together.

"I need to show them, Rosie. I know you think I'm pathetic but it's like it's my mission in this life. Not the next one, of course, I'll be way more elevated for the next one. I just have to show them that it's not all about looks, you know, that they're wrong."

We both knew that it wasn't about proving that looks didn't matter, but that she mattered.

"Rose?" She had this masochistic need to push me until I told the truth.

"Look, you start posting photos and they'll assume it's to get at them. They will. They think everything's about them. You'll just be floating their egos."

"Not if I'm better than them."

I turned and saw the reflection of the fire's flames suddenly flicker in her opaque pupils.

"I have an idea," she said.

Jenny disappeared outside and returned moments later holding a piece of chalk she must have found in the garden. She spoke as she began to use it to scratch thick white lines onto the wooden floorboards. "It's so sad, Rose, we're living like reflections, the shadows of girls who have something we don't. But we can be the influencers, the ones who decide what perfection looks like. We just need people to follow us on Instagram and it'll make it real. It's bloody empowering."

"It won't be real though, will it? It'll be a bunch of pictures telling lies. Can't we just live the lives we want? You think those girls are happy taking pictures of themselves all day? Wake up, Jen. I'm not going to waste my time convincing people my life's worth living instead of living it."

My words were the catchphrases on the T-shirts we'd seen in the giftshops on our walk. But they were better than Jen's mantras. They were true. I felt a heat rising up in me.

"That's something I'd make sacrifices for. An actual life. I'd give my soul for that." I had to catch my breath.

Jenny smiled. "Alright, well, you give your soul for the perfect life, and I'll give mine for the perfect Instagram."

Jenny stood up and looked at the picture she'd drawn, now spanning the entire living-room floor.

"Look familiar?" she asked, fully rhetorically, I knew – she was on one of her tangents. "I'm done making wishes." She threw the chalk on the ground. "It's a pentagram. We're not the angels in this story. We weren't blessed with looks, so things won't come to us. We're going to have to take them."

I clenched my fists. I was no supermodel, but this perpetual need to drag me down with her, to make me feel as ugly as she did, was starting to grate.

"I've been reading into ways to summon the devil," she went on, totally oblivious as per usual to how she made me feel. "This should lure him out. All we have to do is sacrifice something we love. Then we can trade it for the things we want most." She explained it like it wasn't a massive cliché. "I already know what you should sacrifice." She lowered herself to the ground next to me, her big, annoying face inches from mine.

"What?" I asked flatly, anticipating another lecture about how my passion for interior design was dispensable. But she was already distracted, her eyes scanning the constellation on the ground, corroborating, making sure she hadn't missed a thing.

"Candles! So stupid." She got up and wandered around the room, collecting all the candles she could and lining them up along the outside of the pentagram.

"There," she finally said, satisfied, then positioned herself in the centre of the star. "Just let me do the talking. I'll channel for the both of us."

"Don't these pacts always backfire? Isn't that sort of their thing?" I tried, but she was already lost, caught in the web she was spinning, eyes pressed tight and humming. She was loving it. I caught myself wondering how much research she'd done. As if it mattered, as if there was any truth to be found on hocus-pocus.

Jenny's humming intensified, morphing into words: "Let them bend and break to our will. Let us rule them. Let us play them like exquisite violins, until they answer to our every touch, the thrill of our bows. Let us conquer these mortals, oh archfiend." She breathed a deep, raspy breath. "Steal for us the Divine power of creation." She raised her hands to the sky, a devious smirk spreading across her face.

"Let us shape our present, and we will offer you our past and future. Give us the power to live by our sordid desires, and you will have the power to tell the stories we live. We sacrifice to you our legacy."

A sigh passed through the room. I was sure of it. A gust

that almost blew out the candles, then swept through my body: sadness, a feeling of loss. I shivered and held my breath.

Jenny's head flung back. "Give me my Insta-following, oh Angel of Darkness! Grant me my disciples and you shall have yours!" She arched her back, screeching into the empty room like a woman possessed, while I became possessed by the urge to slap her.

Jenny suddenly stopped. Her eyes opened. "I swear to god, I have so many hidden talents."

I stared at her. "You could have checked with me before trading in my past and future."

It didn't actually matter, in the sense that it would have no consequences. What mattered was Jenny's attitude.

"You get the Now. Who cares about the rest?"

"You could have been more specific. You just gave him carte blanche."

"Assuming the devil's a man. Not very feminist."

"Completely beside the point," I snapped. Then, on considering it, "Statistically, he has to be. More men have historically caused more shit. Evil embodied would obviously be a man."

We sat in silence. I reflected on the absurdity of arguing about a supernatural pact I didn't even believe in; while Jenny, I was sure, indulged herself in her latest accomplishment. That in itself was irritating, but what was worse was that she'd intentionally – successfully, as far as she was concerned – signed away the story of my life.

SEVENTEEN

I'm waiting for Ted to come home. My fingers are slipping. I am sliding into the squelch of what I suspect is quicksand. Running out of time. The muddy clump I hang onto suddenly resembles wrinkles on a face; an old, saggy, slimy face. I let go of the clump, turn and run but can't find a way past the multiplications of that same face surrounding me. They stare at me with the same unyielding glare; a glare exactly like Tina's. The faces want to catch me. They open their mouths, trying to eat me whole. I squeeze my eyes closed, try to drag myself back, search for the other dimension, following the memory of light. I scream across the marshes, knowing it's futile, that the dense, stifling world will swallow my voice whole.

The day I moved in with Ted, the day that I'd sorted through our belongings and trimmed away the fat, I'd made a point of severing ties with my past. Our house was a new beginning, not just a new place, but also the start of everything that was going to be important. Adult life. That meant rupture. I'd only kept one relic from my past: a wind-up ballerina clock Dad had given me for my fifth birthday. It was the last good gift he ever gave me. After that, it was all hunting rifles and flat caps. Or he'd just leave it to Mum. Every year, after unwrapping another phallus-shaped parcel, I'd run up to my room and watch the ballerina. I'd listen to the ticking clock, reminding me that it was only a matter of a few more rounds of the clock-face before I'd take the ballerina with me to another home, with another man. A man who would let me be a girl. Now she lived with me and Ted, as planned. She wasn't as central as I'd imagined she would be. Something had driven me to put her on the Victorian side-cabinet in the hall, so that I was only ever reminded of her in passing, or if I really made a point of it.

In my worst moments with Ted, I would sit beside the ballerina clock, and I'd wonder if Ted's indifference was as inevitable as the passing of time. Little girls grow up. Couples drift apart. I'd lean in closer to the clock, listening to the faint whisper of its cogs grinding, remembering the kind of silence it took to hear a clock at work. It took a carpeted children's bedroom of a country estate to really tune in to that sound.

"Christine says driving is fine as long as you take in the scenery. She's not some crazy hippy or anything."

I phased Jenny out as we drove to the house, conjuring up the image of the ballerina, letting myself be lulled into a calmer state by her mechanical twirl. You seek the advice you want, I'd heard somewhere. Not all of us were that lucky. Some had to settle for the only advice they could get. Dinner with Dad – it had been a while.

"Well, that has been a while, hasn't it?" Dad stood looming in the doorway, uncharacteristically greeting me on my arrival. "And you brought Jenny. Jolly good."

I sighed, already dismayed at being reduced to a visit home, and pecked him on the cheek. "Drink?" I demanded.

I made my way to the drawing room and popped open the crystal whisky decanter waiting for me on the mahogany cabinet and poured myself a generous glass. Jenny and Dad followed, sitting themselves down, side-by-side on the Chesterfield sofa facing the fire.

"You shouldn't be drinking like that," Jenny predictably said. "All you need is your body and breath." Jenny turned to Dad. "Your father agrees with me, now. Don't you, Barney?" She elbowed him playfully in his fleshy flank.

Dad cast his eyes down to the floor. I'd never seen him so bashful.

Jenny puffed up. "I've been teaching him yoga."

I almost choked on the fiery scotch that came shooting back up my throat. "Why?" I directed the question at Dad, extending my neck a little to emphasise that I was looking at him, not Jenny. *Shut up, Jenny.*

"I just sensed that he needed spiritual healing. I've really developed a radar for souls in need. I see them with my third eye."

"Shut up, Jenny."

She pressed her lips together, always obedient when we were on my turf. Much more bearable.

"Where's Mum?" I suddenly thought to ask. Dad's face twitched a little, his nose twitching like a rabbit's.

"She's on one of her silly adventures." That's what Dad called the trips Mum took to preserve her sanity in a cold and joyless marriage. They loved each other, in a repressed, bland sort of way, but around her friends, I saw how happy she could be, could have been. She was louder without Dad's booming voice there to drown her out. She was freer without him criticising her every move. I was always surprised to see how her permanently pinched face relaxed in those moments into something almost human.

"Has she been taking a lot of those recently?"

Dad cleared his throat. "I've changed my mind. I will have a scotch. Pour me one, will you Rose?"

I obligingly turned to the cabinet.

"Don't let her dim your light, Barney," Jenny whispered. I poured the drink, hopeful that he'd come to his senses, only to find, when I turned back, Jenny's hand on Dad's arm.

"What are you doing?"

Jenny retracted her hand, taking her time, letting her fingers linger. Dad watched them, unable to drag his eyes away despite my outrage.

"Are you two–?" I couldn't finish the sentence. There were some realities too gruesome for mortal mouths to articulate.

Now they both skulked. Jenny shifted an imperceptible inch away from him, her gaze glued to the ground.

"Does Mum know?"

They remained frozen. A guilty sculpture of a couple fixed in time. I think I preferred them that way.

It was mainly Jenny I was angry at; Dad was just lonely, old and stuck. She was young, had a world of options, was just doing this for the same reason she did anything in her pathetically recursive existence: to upset me. I momentarily considered throwing something at her, thought the crystal could do some serious damage to her big, obnoxious skull. But I was already tinkering on the edge, I realised. Ted would definitely testify against me, and I'd end up in prison as the broken, manic housewife. Another casualty in the annuls of psychobitches. The Stepford Wife defunct. I wouldn't give any of them that satisfaction.

"It doesn't even matter," I said, my voice unnervingly steady even to my own ears. "You and Mum haven't been happy since, well, ever."

Dad looked up at me, his eyes expressive for the first time, well, ever. Emotion: sad. Maybe even a little guilty. I'd always wondered if he knew how his apathy had made me feel rejected from birth. And now it seemed that he did. For the first time in my life, he was penetrable to me; I could see into him. Jenny had done what my mum never had – she'd softened him up.

I watched the emotions play out through micro-tensions around his eyes, so small it took a daughter to be able to read them, but I did. After sadness and guilt came surprise, followed by suspicion as he tried to suss out my intentions, then resolve, as he finally decided to take his little girl for her word.

"I'm going to make us dinner."

He roasted lamb, with rosemary. We drank red wine, even Jenny, and we talked and laughed just like the night after the hunt all that time ago. It was so familiar, I was almost completely transported to a time before Ted, and before my childhood friend had become my father's mistress. None of that seemed important. In this time portal, only meaty juices and deep aroma mattered; only glowing faces and stomachs told the truth.

After dinner, Dad made a fire, and Jenny and I lay down on the rug, side by side, like that other night so long ago, in the Lake District, before she'd cursed my existence and broken our friendship, back when illicit affairs would have been the height of betrayal. A moment I suddenly dared to believe could exist as long as I wanted it to.

EIGHTEEN

I'm waiting for Ted to come home. Because I love him. Deeply. And it is an honest love. He knows me in ways nobody else ever could. He knows me as a fresh-faced newborn in a whole new world. He knows me for the stripped-back self I am, without a history of privilege to define me. That has to be worth fighting for. I squeeze my eyes so tightly that darkness turns to blotchy light. I'm back in the room.

Slowly, the shadowy woods of my mind recede, to be replaced by the much less intimidating sight of the tuft of hair between my legs. I blink. Suddenly, it isn't so bold of a statement. Slightly underwhelming, in fact. Despite my resolution to remain frozen, I smile slightly, the plaster in the corners of my mouth cracking at the thought that there had been a time when I'd believed that it was just that sprout of hair at the centre of our contention. How naïve I'd been, to think that Ted's attraction could hang on a single pubic thread. It is both comforting and terrifying to know that it depends on so much more. To know that there is so much more to personal upkeep, but at the same time, for that very reason, also so much more to keep Ted enticed. It isn't just pubic hair – it is skin, toenails, eyebrows and teeth. It is empowering and daunting to know that I am embroiled in a lifelong battle to maintain the lady-magnet that will keep Ted drawn to me.

Jenny's fingers moved through the sheepy plush towards me. Our faces were hot from the fire. Dad had gone to "do the washing up", by which he meant smoke a cigar in solitude as he processed his feelings about the night. We were alone. Her hand touched my arm. I wondered for a moment how many boundaries she was planning to cross. She'd got off surprisingly lightly so far. Maybe I'd inspired her to push on. Defiling me was probably her Holy Grail, it suddenly occurred to me, or her Nirvana or whatever she called her narcissistic ambitions. If it had crossed her mind, she seemed to think better of it, letting her hand go limp on my shoulder as we continued to stare into the flames.

"You know what I've been thinking?" Jenny suddenly said. I didn't answer. I never had to. "That maybe Dad dying was my sacrifice. You know, for the pact."

"Don't be ridiculous," was all I could muster.

"He was my past, you know, and my future. He was going to decide it all. He hated the yoga. He would never have let me turn the house into a studio. He would've waited till I married someone vaguely suitable, whatever that means, and then let me manage the house, birth heirs to the throne." She said it like it was a joke. "He would have made sure of it. So, you know, he was my childhood, my past, and he would've decided my future. Maybe that's why the devil took him."

"A generous devil, then. He gave you your story back."

Jenny shrugged. If she'd been cursed, she wouldn't have known it. I envied Jenny; everything was self-affirming to her.

At worst, something she could spin into a victim story to build her following.

"Well, you haven't paid your price at all," she said, squinting at me. It was, ridiculously, an accusation. As if this was a game you could cheat at.

"Because it's not real."

"It is real. I can feel it." She turned back to the fire. "I think a part of me wanted you to pay the price."

Her honesty sent a jolt through me. I froze.

"I think maybe that's why I let Barney, you know–"

A jut of bile escaped my still-bulging stomach, acid reflux mixed with old hate mixed with remnants of lamb.

"At first, that is. Now I really do love him. I think maybe the kind of love I want is masochistic. Where you know you'll get hurt. It's like I need to feel I've sacrificed everything for it to count. It's some kind of paradox, like the more of me I'm giving up, the more I exist. God, I'm deep."

I looked at her. She was deluded beyond words. Yet she got to walk around believing she knew the meaning of sacrifice. It was infuriating, how I still pitied her. Something about her sincerity always displaced my own pain with hers, let our dysfunctional friendship continue for all infinity.

Dad entered the room smelling of sweet smoke. He sat down on the Chesterfield of my childhood, legs crossed, now pensive. The way I knew him to be. I wanted to curl up next to him, but something stopped me. Maybe it was the sudden tension I sensed in Jenny's body, her imminent movement. She got up and went to sit beside him, arm draped over his shoulder – him, her part-replacement father, part-faded semblance of a lover; her, his part-replacement wife, part-daughter who stuck by him. A sad picture if ever I saw one. I knew it was time to leave.

NINETEEN

I'm waiting for Ted to come home. I am, by now, seriously bored. I consider turning on the television but decide that would cheapen the gesture. The point is to wait, to prove my undying commitment and affection to him, not continue the drag of mindless distraction I now realise I've been fixating on. Instead, I try to find items in the room to centre me. I've spent all this time creating a visually pleasing room, I may as well reap the rewards.

I land my gaze on the canopic jars lined up on the bookcase. Limestone carved in the shape of four gods; facsimiles, of course, but I love them all the same. I'd always imagined, especially at the height of our arguing, that if I killed Ted, or even if he died of natural causes, that's where I'd keep his ashes. Forever trapped inside the symbol of a time he knew nothing about. History, to Ted, is *Game of Thrones*. He doesn't know that the Ancient Egyptians assigned a god to each organ: the baboon-god for the lungs, the jackal for the stomach, human for the liver, falcon for the intestines. He doesn't know that there isn't a jar for the heart, that symbolic core of our humanity, and so wouldn't understand how this is fitting, given that this is the organ I am trying to win back. I scan them each from top to bottom, the way Jenny told me you should scan your own body when you meditate – the curved tops of their heads, their beaks and snouts, wide shoulders, hieroglyphs in an inky trail of whisps and dashes down their chests. By the time my eyes reach their feet, I feel different, relaxed. I zoom out and take them all in again: the baboon blinks, opens its thick lips, speaking on behalf of the lungs.

"Breathe, my goddess," he says. "Let air fill you and revive you. It's all you need to live."

I frown at him. His lips shut, snapping the way Jenny's did when I shushed her. His lashes look suddenly longer, thicker, his big face strangely effeminate.

"Breathe, Rosie, it's such a natural high." It is Jenny. I should have known – she'd been lurking here on my shelf all this time, waiting for her moment to stick her thick snout into my life. There was no end to her scheming. A shudder passes through the other jars as they all slowly awaken. Their eyes flutter open, and their faces turn from beasts to beauties. These are the girls I follow on Instagram. The falcon, god of the intestines, is now the it-girl from school, Belinda, who tells me she'd always suspected I had poor gut health. The stoic human turns into my mother, pert as ever in a Chanel suit, telling me Ted is a drinker, that he has it coming, by which I assume she means liver failure. But it is the jackal who hurts the most. My guru, my goddess: Mrs Ladyfriend. She sears me with the words I'd always dreaded, that I am too fat to be an interior designer, because looks do matter, no matter what I keep telling myself; I *am* the product, and I will never sell. The row of ladies wriggle and jibe, spitting out dust like I know they will my ashes.

*

What had I been thinking, expecting comfort from my dad? I'd mistaken familiarity for integrity. My issues with Ted had made me nostalgic. But he and Jenny had reminded me, in fact, I was grateful – they'd given me a concrete reason never to speak to them again. Only, who did that leave me with?

I drove through the dark country lanes. Just me in my Mini Cooper among the rolling English hills. Although, in the thick of the night, it could have been anywhere – Italy, Spain, southern France. What did it matter in your darkest hour where you came from? The feeling of my stomach lurching on every hump in the landscape would have been the same anywhere in the world. Gut-wrenching loneliness was universal. Only Ted didn't seem to feel it. His own ego seemed to trump any loss he might have felt, seemed more important to him than the dream of happiness we'd once shared.

It occurred to me as I was driving that perhaps I'd been waiting for Ted long before we'd even met. Waiting for a man with the capacity to love, a man to build a different kind of life with. And I'd never really found him. I thought I had, but now it was clear that Ted had just been a night-time hallucination. That's the problem with visionaries; sometimes they find it hard to discern their visions from realities, hopes from the facts.

I dreamt about his mother that night. I dreamt that she was trying to help me. Wendy, my archvillain, suddenly on my side. She descended before me in her tracksuit, white wings strapped to her back as she was hoisted down on a rope, awkwardly, like in some amateurish Nativity play.

"Don't be too hard on him, darlin'. He'll come around. He always does. Just gets himself in a muddle sometimes. Nothing to do with you, dear, nothing to do with you…"

A weight lifted off my chest. Divine reassurance, that's all I needed. Faith that he'd come back to me. That I hadn't ruined my only chance at happiness. For a moment, I was calm. I let Wendy whisk me off the ground, lay me on a cloud, and put me to sleep. I nestled into the cotton-wool warmth, held in a mother's nest.

Only when I woke up – to my empty house, a pallete of blues and silvers that now seemed like a prophetic choice for this cold era of abandonment – I remembered that there was no woman holding me; that, in actual fact, I'd shunned the only friend who had tried to be my ally. Tina was probably upset. But she was also wise, patient. She'd lived through enough to know where there was hope, who would come to their senses. I could always trust her to see the bigger picture.

She'd told me that I wanted love more than I wanted a career, and that, to me, had been the worst possible insult. Only now, reminded of the selfish actions and broken bonds that had made my life, I knew she was right. I wanted love more than success. I wanted Ted more than Instagram. I wanted Tina's magic over Jenny's.

TWENTY

I'm waiting for Ted to come home. The canopic jars finally go to sleep. Their penetrating eyeballs close, then ossify, their faces ancient once again. The clock informs me that my time in the stocks has taken only a few minutes, but I feel frayed like a gnawed-on piece of chicken. Perhaps this is more than I can take. Maybe there are other ways to get Ted back. Perhaps simply giving up my Instagram would suffice. That thought would have seemed harrowing, impossible, just a few hours ago, but now seems like a cleaner, brighter path. A sacrifice less total. Less dark and lonely.

I scold myself. This is nothing. I've seen true darkness, the darkness that lurks at the back of my mind. This is nothing in comparison. The dark of the night is a mortal darkness; one I know will pass. I just have to remind myself of the world I am in. I move my hand, down my body, just to feel the temperature of my skin, just to prove to myself that I am still a living, beating thing. I stroke the side of my thigh, smooth, shaven, then push my finger into the flesh. I sigh. It has a plumpness that reassures me. I'm still here. I bring the finger to my nose and sniff the smell of lavender and lotion: a memory of the bath that had warmed me before I'd cooled, reminding me that this same body connects me to that moment, that I've existed between then and now.

Tina opened the door and smiled. I was nervous. Armpits sweating. Strange prickle in my gut like the itch of a tapeworm.

"Tina, I'm sorry."

She said nothing, stepped aside, and indicated for me to come in. I walked into the living room, to find that the card table was still there. As promised. I stood in the doorway, gratefully taking in the scene, then cried.

Unphased by my tears, Tina gently put her hand on my back and led me to my familiar chair.

"I'll fetch the tea." She disappeared behind her room divider. I watched her silhouette as she made her preparations. The swooping sleeves of a kimono, the elegant lines of her fingers as they lifted the teapot, filled it with water, stacked on a strainer and filled it with crunchy tea leaves. It was a slow, controlled dance; sombrely optimistic, as if performing the ritual was accepting the sadness at the centre of all life.

Tina emerged from behind the partition. From moth to butterfly, her shadow burst into colour – fuchsia, magenta and indigo. She floated steadily towards me with her silky wings, carrying her pot in her hands, until she came to rest on her stool, where she had sat all those weeks ago, like nothing had ever changed. Only she was brighter.

"I'm sorry about how we left things, dear," she said, pouring the tea. "It was my mistake. I committed the self-same atrocity of which I wanted to warn you, you see. I tried to force the hand of the universe, to warn you prematurely, before your alignment, your metamorphosis." Her emerald eyes sparkled euphorically. I wanted to put them where my heart was. "Fortune puts us in these binds."

I nodded, as always with Tina, only partially understanding. Only partially understanding, too, the sense of shift within me.

Tina placed the tips of her fingers on the edge of the coffee table, as if presenting me with her nails – finely manicured, of course, lacquered today in plum-purple. She hovered them just above the table, closing her eyes, quietly concentrated, searching for the place we'd left off.

"Let us remind ourselves," she spoke as she swaddled her emeralds in wrinkled eyelids, hiding them from me. "We saw stagnation in your past, a block, obsolescence. The Three of Wands captured that nicely."

I nodded, biting my lip.

"And we saw retreat in your present. The Hermit, a card which when reversed signifies isolation, withdrawal." She opened her eyes and looked at me, ensuring that this time I would accept the truths she spoke. She reached her hand towards the first of the final row of cards, about to flip it over, then hesitated.

"A word of clarification. The Hermit has his virtues. His aims are noble. He carries his lantern through the snowy mountain peaks seeking spiritual mastery, growth and accomplishments. It is a path of self-discovery, a venturing into unchartered territory towards heightened awareness. Inside his lantern is the six-pointed star, the Seal of Solomon."

The seal seemed familiar. The chalky lines that Jenny had scrawled on the floor the night of that other ritual still lurked hazily in my subconscious. Here was another star, with one additional point, maybe indicating a way out. Tina looked up at me, noting with surprise, I could feel, my calm sense of recognition. I soaked up what felt like maternal pride.

"Only, she forgets that her lantern illuminates a narrow path, that her steps guide her through a landscape but never reveal to her the entire journey. In order to know what lies ahead, all she can do is take the next steps. You see, isolation at its best is exploration, not stagnation. It requires an open mind."

My mind was wide open. I had to cling on to the two mortal companions I had left in this world. I had no choice but to spread my cerebral flaps to the power of the universe. Tina waited a few moments, then smiled.

"Good." She nodded and moved her hovering hands down. She turned the card.

We both gasped.

The hunched-over figure of a hooded man carrying a lantern containing the six-pointed star, illuminating only his next step. The Hermit had returned.

"How is this possible?" Tina, for the first time ever, looked flustered.

"There's a second Hermit?"

"There is only one Hermit in a pack." Tina's gems scoured the other rows of cards, defying all ritual and flipping the final two. Having taken them all in, she finally came to rest. "They got jumbled," she huffed, wagging her wide sleeves to bring air flow to her hot and bothered body.

I looked down at the cloaked, bearded man, suddenly stifling the urge to laugh. It was somehow farcical that it would be the image of an aging, fading old codger of a man to try to claim my fate.

Tina glared at me. "You would be wise not to mock the tarot. Even a botched reading has consequence, in fact, may unleash it across constellations far and wide, ones I am unable to access."

She tapped her chin pensively.

"I always knew it."

"What?"

"This is serious."

"Tell me, Tina." I reached for her arm, but she pulled back. "Please."

She straightened the folds in her kaftan. "You have a tendency towards fossilization."

Something moved inside of me. That same twitch at the point where my gut met my bowels. The wisp of a slimy tail, the slither of a worm-like tendril. A snake, perhaps.

Tina gazed down pensively at the cards, a purple finger-nail tapping the side of that angular chin. "You must be very careful," she said as if to herself. "You have touched a pressure point. Equilibrium is paramount."

"Paramount to what?" I could no longer afford not to know.

"You must not cause more unrest. Be good to Ted. Don't move the furniture. Don't go anywhere. Don't do anything. Keep the peace, my dear. There may be more than your life at stake."

"Like what, Tina? Please be clear. Tell me exactly." I stared down at the Hermit, his face melting, nose drooping into the semblance of a maniacal jester.

Tina raised her head high, her emeralds taunting me with the comfort they once brought. "Like the order of the universe."

TWENTY-ONE

I'm waiting for Ted to come home. The fuse in the lamp has blown. With the lightbulb extinguished, the room feels even darker than before. The cold sucks the moisture of the lotions from my skin, then the oil from my foundation, turning my face and neck into cracked desert earth. I can't risk going up to fix it, not now; Ted's arrival really is imminent. I've worked so hard, waited so long. My face was never the pièce de resistance anyway, and my body is still intact; that is the most important thing. Smooth, naked, pure: my body is where his eyes will go to the moment he walks in. Men are impatient like that. Up to the woman to show the restraint they can't. Up to the woman to redeem them. Up to the woman to fill the cracks they leave with her fleshy filler. It isn't the face that matters. It is the body and soul.

I sense a flickering in the corner of my eye. It is the floor lamp in the corner, a vintage lampshade that I'd found at an antique fair, frilly and kitsch in all the right ways. Mysteriously, the lightbulb had come on, electricity firing through the cable connecting it to the wall in audible static bursts. I move my head fractionally to look at the lamp. She opens her googly eyeballs, revealing emeralds. The pink of the lampshade in the deep glow of the lightbulb is fleshy, like skin, capillaries darting across its surface in all directions, blood visibly pulsating throughout.

"Tina?" I say. I'm sure it's her. "What happened to you?"

Lips pop out of the tightly spun film; thin, elongated, spreading wider into a wobbly smile.

"My darling." Her eyelashes flutter, coated thick in mascara. "You have done well!"

I look away, bashful. "It's nothing."

"It is *not* nothing!" She is stern. "It takes dedication and discipline to scrub up the way you just did. These are both virtuous qualities in a woman."

She's right, I know, but I also know that she'd say it was unladylike to brag.

"You're going to have to remind yourself how far you've come to get through this next bit. Don't lose morale, my dear!" The lampshade winks at me.

"You mean it'll get more difficult?" I'm distraught.

"Everything only ever becomes more difficult. When it comes to relationships, where you are is always the easy bit. Remember that. But there's no point keeping track. Give and don't expect to gain. Give and expect nothing back, and you cannot lose, Rosalind. Do you understand me?"

I nod. I think I do.

"It is, in fact, the most emancipated life goal. Women today don't understand. When you give, selflessly, you are in control, my dear. Your destiny becomes your own."

I wonder for a second if control is, in the end, really the same as freedom. But then the lightbulb fizzles and dies. And I am alone again, in a silent room, and those thoughts suddenly seem entirely irrelevant.

*

Tina sent me off with a peck on the cheek. Strangely maternal. Then I went home.

I opened the door and stopped, taking in, as I always did, the ambience of the room. It was good to take a moment every day to feel the effects of your interior. That's how you sensed if it was working – and when it was time to change. Pathetic fallacy, they taught us at school, as part of their attempt to discredit Romanticism and, at an all-girls school, to try to deter bright young women from premature "sexual relations" (as the unbelievably dusty old teachers called it), maybe romance too. The Romantic poets projected their feelings onto their environment, they said; not the other way around. The sky wasn't really darker than it was yesterday, only your mood was. The literary version of "It's all in your head". I never understood why causality mattered – the practical question, to me, seemed what to do when you were down in the dumps. Sometimes the answer was as simple as a coat of paint.

Today, the blues and greys were serene. Surprising, really, considering the report of existential threat Tina had just divulged. But there was a softness to the room, so meditative. I could practically smell the eucalyptus. I wandered in, dropped my keys on the kitchen table, and sighed, feeling my lungs ache as they expanded, as if it was the first breath I'd taken in far too long. For a moment, I thought my pathetic fallacy had taken over. Spa music came echoing in soft cadences from somewhere in my subconscious with eerie clarity. Only, as I listened, the source seemed to be not inside my own head, but upstairs. Could the impossible have happened? Could Ted be listening to spa music?

I climbed the stairs and looked for the source of activity. Light shone under the door to the bedroom, left slightly ajar. It had a quality I knew well. Unpretentious, nonchalant, classic: the glow of candlelight. I tiptoed across the landing and peered in through the opening. The impossible manifested before me in a form I could never have imagined. Ted was crouched on the ground amidst a sea of tealights, head bowed, hands woven together in prayer. I watched him as he muttered to himself, his brow furrowed in concentration. I tried to imagine what he could possibly be saying; he'd never been this verbose around me. Perhaps this was him grasping for straws in response to our crisis. Or maybe he'd always had hidden depths I didn't know. It wasn't the worst thing. I had been telling him he needed male friends he could actually talk to. Now here he was, enacting my advice so creatively, revealing himself to be more than I even knew. My pious Ted, talking to God.

After a while, Ted unclasped his hands. He looked at them; stared into them as if God had only just given him hands and he was looking at them for the first time. I tried to imagine the picture he saw. Maybe he had a forest too. His probably wasn't as unruly as mine, just the sprawl of lines in his palms: deep grooves that branched into twigs and strokes, thin as feathers. Perhaps, when he looked deeper, flowers sprouted from the tangle of vines – bursts of fuchsia, tangerine and lime blossom. Perhaps, after a while, when he had settled his gaze and let it sink through the canopy to the damp earth, through the shrubbery, perhaps he'd find a still pool of water. There, he'd watch the lilies hovering over glass, their roots pristinely preserved in the prism below; a scene perfectly still, carp not swimming, but frozen in suspended animation, mouths wide, their final breath captured in bubbles of infinitude. Ted's forest, unlike mine, was probably a nice place to be.

Perhaps he'd wonder how he'd never seen it all before. Knots, tangles, complexity. All of it captivating, magical; all of it true. Perhaps it reminded him of the knot of neurons in his own head – equally complex, equally a world for him to explore. Perhaps, he'd reason, it was worth just every once in a while opening up that hand always braced to prove your masculinity, unclasping your palms and taking in your vulnerable humanity. Because it is beautiful, because it is so much more than being a man.

I watched him lower his hands to the floor, waited for him to descend back down to Earth. I waited a little longer, then opened the door and walked in.

"What's all of this?" I asked in my most unassuming voice. "Getting romantic?" I added for good measure.

Ted looked up at me, not as perturbed by my sudden appearance as I'd expected. Not at all ashamed, it seemed, of revealing such a sensitive side.

"Come here," was all he said, and he opened his arms to me. I went and joined him in the bed of light, let him wrap himself around me, squeezing me into his chest with such force it had to be love. I stayed there for a while, cheek covering two buttons in the row down the front of his shirt. I ignored the discomfort of the circle imprints, focusing as much as I could on the smell of his sweat in synthetic cloth. The scent of the man I loved. I inhaled until his arm hugged around my face too tight for me to breathe.

I gently tugged at his sleeve, asking him to move it, but his grip stayed strong.

"I need some air," I tried, but for a moment he only squeezed harder. "Ted!"

I used both hands to release the clamp of his arm. He finally pulled it back, just enough to move his hands to my face, tilting my chin up, presenting my lips to him. He moved in to kiss me.

I writhed in his grip. "No." But he squeezed my cheeks together and pushed his face against mine. "I want to talk first, Ted. I want to apologise."

My face still sandwiched between his hands, he moved onto his knees, silently pushing me down as he lowered himself on top of me. He spread his hands, one either side of my head, his legs, one either side of mine, spanning himself across me like a spatchcock chicken. He rubbed his crotch against me, dipping down then pulling back, teasing me in the intermittent moments of space between us with the possibility of release.

I watched him consider where to go next. He moved his hand under my cardigan and, using a single finger, traced a line down my belly, then pushed that same finger down my trousers, just barely touching my clit with the very tip, when he stopped. He pulled his finger back. I felt his body soften, the anger, or whatever had been driving him, drain from his muscles. He got up; his gorilla silhouette hovered over me a few moments more. I wondered how much harm he wished me. How much he wanted to hurt me. Which he hated more: my body or my soul. Finally, he coughed, turned, and left the room.

He left me there, on the floor, catching my breath, and my thoughts, watching the tealights burn as the sun set outside, flames working their way through wax, leaving only sooty marks on a coal-black canvas.

TWENTY-TWO

I'm waiting for Ted to come home. Once, when I'd done an online yoga class with Jenny, there was a point at the end where we had to lay entirely still. "Savasana," the woman in spandex had called it. There was something transcendent, I remember, about resisting the urge to move, as though your consciousness is suddenly lifted when you ignore its passing needs. I levitated above my body like it was a familiar friend but not me. I'd used the same technique the times Ted had touched me after that one night. It worked, most of the time, made me feel less alone in those quasi-intimate moments. I hope to apply the same discipline now, only I can't seem to settle into quiet observation. My consciousness refuses to leave my body, seems stuck to it. My mind travels instead in thick, gloopy form, like cement across my skin, basting my body in sticky paste. I watch my new hide wrap itself around me – tight, like a lover's embrace.

I clutched my phone tight in my hand as I descended the stairs, 999 already keyed in, my thumb over the dial button. Prepared. I no longer knew what he was capable of; he'd horrifically surpassed all expectations. I inched towards the doorway and peeked in. He was sitting on the chaise longue, bare feet outstretched and resting on a stool, beer in his hand. He'd moved the television from its spot facing the sofa, so that he could watch it from his new location.

I entered the room – slow, mousy. He looked up and smirked, his face ominously lit by the glaring reflection from the screen.

"Think I was too harsh, babe, this chair's pretty comfy."

I stared at him, unsure what to do. He seemed unhinged. I turned to go back upstairs.

"What's for dinner?"

I froze. I wondered for a moment what he'd do if I refused to cook for him. A silly thought, I quickly told myself. He wasn't dangerous. He'd stopped himself before it had gone too far. He was just angry, and that was understandable; we'd been fighting. Things had been difficult between us, and men just have a different way of expressing themselves. More physical. Ted wasn't a monster, but a real man. My man. I *wanted* to have dinner with him. It had been so long, and he'd finally come around. I heated us up a vegetarian curry.

I spooned the curry into bowls, added yoghurt and naan for good measure, sprinkled coriander on top. I took a picture and posted it with the hashtags #foodporn #foodie #food #foodbowl #healthyfood #healthylifestyle #housewifelife #housewifey #femininity #food #netflixandchill #sex. Then I brought the Instagrammable bowls to Ted on the chaise longue. I sat down beside him.

"What're you watching?" I asked him, trying to simulate postcoital vibes of the consensual variety. This could be the evening we resolved our differences. It could be the evening Ted expressed himself and we finally cleared the air; and the day I started to accommodate him, let him eat on my pristine new piece of furniture. The day we both compromised.

"*Game of Thrones*. Not very girly. You won't like it."

"Try me," I said, ever so sweetly.

He was good, he was kind – so generous that he restarted the series from the first episode. He was right, I didn't like it. But I liked watching it with him. I watched a woman getting raped from behind by a man about four times her size in sub-hygienic conditions and it put everything in perspective for me. What had just transpired between us, in comparison, was poppycock.

TWENTY-THREE

I'm waiting for Ted to come home. I'm not sure if my ashen grey body is a figment of my imagination, or just the way a naked body looks in the depths of the night, but I'm not in the right frame of mind to decide. Reality or fantasy can be determined later, after Ted gets home. When I know what the future holds. I try to imagine the world beyond the room. Somewhere, above the concrete ceiling, there are stars. Bright, swollen gems of promise that I used to be able to see from the grounds at night. Not in the suburbs. Not from the crowded streets of houses pouring out artificial light. Besides, you'd look like a madwoman standing in the middle of the street trying to peer through the haze. So it is hard sometimes to get any kind of perspective; easy to forget that what we've created here, what we've assembled using a combination of bought plastics and antiques, is all just a simulation of a world, something we've made. Disposable. That with some glue and new materials I could do it all again, with someone else, somewhere else. Better.

It seemed appropriate to consult Tina on Ted's uncharacteristic behaviour, given that there could be metaphysical motions at play. Perhaps she could assure me that, as I already suspected, he'd been possessed, led astray by forces beyond his control. That once this astrological movement, or whatever it was that implored him, had reconciled itself, he'd return to the placid character I'd always known. And loved.

Tina was not shocked, nor surprised. She was calm like I wanted her to be.

"We cannot hold the forces responsible, darling. Must I remind you, that's not how this works. You youngsters and your self-centred ways."

"I don't know what to do."

"You must do exactly what I've been telling you for much too long now. You must take responsibility."

"How can I possibly take responsibility for what he did?"

Tina sniggered. "Yes, how could you possibly."

She'd been waiting for this. She wanted me in pain, to turn me into a destitute old bag like her.

"I don't know how things worked back in your day," I said, "but these days, rape is considered a crime. On the man's part."

I heard myself call what Ted had done to me "rape". I'd wanted to write it off as misguided foreplay. I'd wanted Tina to reassure me. But now I'd said it, now I'd said that toxic word, there would never the end. It was always contagious. I'd unleashed the plague into my sunshine-coated life, and it was going to leave it unrecognisable.

Tina's face turned steely cold.

"You're right, dear, you don't know how things worked back in my day. But I'll have you know that if I'd whined and moaned, perhaps then what transpired between me and my Stanley would have been deemed a crime just as it is today. But I chose not to. I kept my mouth shut. I stuck by him because when you take a person you take all of them and you help them. You don't blame them. You don't make it all about you."

"But it's my body," I stammered.

"It's yours for this life, and you ought to be grateful, and make the best of it."

I crossed my arms, infuriatingly aware that I looked to her like a sulky child. I didn't care. Anyone else would have agreed with me. Even Mum would have been outraged. Ted may not have raped me, but he'd made me feel like he could. His finger had pointed towards his intention. He'd wanted to scare me, hurt me. Why did that not count in Tina's relationship tally?

"Life isn't perfect, you must have heard."

"I wouldn't say a rape-free relationship is an ideal exactly." I pouted.

"Abandon yourself. Look up. Your body, your mind, they are just one reality. There is a world beyond, a universe. It's so big, Rosalind. It's so magnificent. There is so much more than what you are clinging on to for dear life."

"He broke my trust."

"Look outwards. Take the pressure off Ted, and he will stop acting out."

"So it's my fault? That's really what you're saying?"

"It doesn't matter whose fault it is. It's up to you to coax him back. Men feel paradoxically emasculated when they go too far in asserting their dominance."

"Or what? He feels guilty for what he's done? Good."

"Or you will lose him, and perhaps more."

A weight inside of me dropped, pulled me down. There wasn't more. Ted was everything. Last night I'd lost the Ted I thought I knew. That had been enough to petrify me. He'd reminded me of what I might lose. Maybe that had been his plan, which would make his actions less vindictive, maybe even sensible. I'd seen another side to him that night after all: pious Ted. The Ted who prayed, perhaps for a better future. Maybe for us. A Ted who was desperately reaching, trying all he could to make things right.

"I want him back, Tina, but I'm tired of playing games. Why can't I just talk to him?"

Tina rolled her eyes. "Ah yes, the talking cure. Another millennial favourite." She raised her authoritative chin. "I should remind you that this situation you find yourself in transcends the relationship. You must take care. The universe is in a volatile state. You risk losing yourself as well as Ted. I am not speaking metaphorically."

I didn't dare ask how one could lose herself literally. Thoughts of dark voids and Jenny's curse withheld me.

"The problem isn't communication. The problem is that you are unwilling to play your part."

"And that means manipulating him?"

"That entails giving him what he needs. Pride will destroy you, Rosalind. Come to me when you're ready to put that aside, or I can't help you."

Tina was my curse. She was trying to claim my story just as I was growing my following, just as I really wanted to fix things with Ted, trying to make it resemble her own. I wouldn't let her do that. I wasn't going to surrender my future to her, not for something that only barely resembled rape.

TWENTY-FOUR

I'm waiting for Ted to come home. My body, from the outside, looks still. That much is possible with sheer determination. Inside, however, there is only turmoil. Heart pounding, neurons firing, stomach cramping and, most annoyingly of all, bladder bursting. The doctor had called my incessant need to urinate "housewife's bladder". At first, I'd worried that it was something serious, but the disorder, he explained, is very prevalent amongst housewives who, in the absence of sufficient stimulating activity, find themselves attending the bathroom before they really need to, conditioning themselves into neurotic patterns of urination. Easily rectified by resisting the urge to go. This is a test if ever there was one, maybe also my cure. My abdomen aches, the tissue expanding into a turgid balloon. I try to imagine that the bulge of my inflated tummy contains a baby not my bladder, that the discomfort is the most natural thing in the world, the cost of motherhood. I send tender thoughts to the bump, tell myself I am nurturing it on Ted's behalf too, carrying out my end of the bargain, so that we might share a future.

I woke up to a stain. I'd noticed it the night before while we'd been watching TV, but I didn't want to ruin the moment by getting all "neurotic", as I knew Ted would describe it. So I'd contained myself as I watched him smear his greasy naan-stained hands on my prize acquisition. Let him do it and hoped that it wouldn't infiltrate the fabric and that, with enough soap and water and what Wendy called "elbow grease", I'd be able to get it out the following day. I'd learnt all my cleaning techniques from her; it was one of the few things we could bond over. The Instagram housewives only showed you the "after", see; never the "before". God forbid the "during".

It had grown bigger. Offensive. Something had to be done. I armed myself with baking powder and a pair of rubber gloves and kneeled down at the site of the stain, digging into the cushion with all my strength. Evil thoughts rose like undulating tides within me: thoughts of vengefulness, thoughts of blame. Weren't you meant to grow in a relationship? To prop each other up? I felt like I was shrinking. My sense of style had matured, that was one thing, but that was all my own doing. What had Ted really done for me?

I looked around the room, confirming what I already knew: it was all me. Every last part of it was my work, my blood and sweat and elbow grease. His only contribution was the ugly blemish that hung in the corner – his *Game of Thrones* figurines on his little shelf. I'd managed to ignore them for so long, had worked around them in the photos I took as though avoiding an accidental scratch in the woodwork. But they were malicious. Ted had always made a point to tend to them. They were juvenile, pathetic, but received more love than I ever did. My heart beat aggressively against the inside of my ribcage. It's not important, I told myself. Remember Tina's words. Get rid of the stain. Maintain the balance. This, us, our relationship – all just blips in a universe, a universe that wasn't all about me.

In the midst of my scrubbing, Mum called. She never called. I answered with a sense of foreboding.

"He's done the dirty on me, Rosie!" She blubbered. Mum never blubbered. I couldn't help but scoff.

"You don't say that, Mum."

"Men don't cheat on me either," she screeched into my ear.

I sighed. "All men cheat."

"That's ridiculous. You must stop with these vulgar sayings." Reprimanding me seemed to calm her down.

"Alright, well, if that's all."

"No, wait!" Her voice shaky again. Pathetic. "It's that tart, Jenny. Your little friend. The one who always wore the low-cut tops."

"I remember Jenny, Mum." A strange sensation came over me. A pang in my side like a forgotten friend. I suspected it was guilt, perhaps, the slightest of regrets that I hadn't told my own mother about the affair making a mockery of her life. Although I owed her nothing.

She paused for a few extended moments, panting down the phone like she always did. Irritating. I could almost feel her tea-stained breath in my earhole.

"It's a phone, not a breathalyser, Mum. How many times must I tell you?"

"Did you know?"

I paused and put my sponge down, considered for a moment whether our relationship was worth lying for. "I didn't know how hurt you'd be."

"But you did know? About your father and the hussy?"

"What century are we in?"

"Answer me, Rosalind."

Her steady voice transported me to childhood, to shoelaces untied and thank-yous forgotten. To feeling cornered. "Yes."

"So you betrayed me too."

"Don't be so dramatic."

"No, darling, it's not dramatic. You ignore me for years, abandon the home I tried to build for you despite your father being no help at all. Instead you go and live with that dollop of a man, a man you knew I didn't approve of. And then, as if that's not enough, you go and drag your parents down with you, like the childhood I gave you, we gave you, meant nothing, like you want to see it destroyed, like you hate me. It's vile, what you did, Rosalind, absolutely beastly."

I'd never heard her so impassioned. Rather beautiful. People really surprise you with their poetry in moments of rage, I was beginning to discover. I was faintly affected, somewhere in a far-off place, in a time before I stopped caring. Yes, I was sure of it; a version of me felt for her. But we were strangers now. Which meant my reputation was at stake – something she'd taught me, in fact. I had to stand my ground.

"You can't blame me for your failed marriage," I said.

She huffed. She always huffed when she was doubting herself.

"I mean, honestly, Mother, you've been neglecting him for years. You of all people should know that it takes work to keep a marriage going. That's something your generation believes, isn't it? I don't know when you felt he stopped caring but it was probably around the time you started going off with your friends instead of making it work with him."

It felt good, teaching my mother the lessons she'd utterly failed to impart to me.

"He had an affair, Rosalind. No, never mind, it doesn't even warrant the term. You can't have an affair with a child. He did the dirty!"

"Stop saying that," I snapped.

"He's in the wrong, not me."

"It doesn't matter. You have to fix it. You're the wife."

My breathing grew heavier, faster. My head light, vision blurred. Focus on the stain.

"I don't have to do anything," she said. "I'm a sixty-year-old woman and times have changed. I've had my child; I've done my duty. I want to enjoy the years I have left. There are men who still find me desirable, you know? Younger men, even."

"None of that will matter if Dad doesn't want you."

"I won't be a prisoner any longer. I've spent my life in shackles!" She was manic.

I clasped onto the sofa, trying to steady myself in the now nauseating swirl of the room.

"Mother, do what you want. Just don't talk to me about tarnishing your legacy, or whatever. You did that yourself." I threw the phone on the floor and leaned over the chaise longue, heaving, staring deep into the damp patch I'd been scrubbing, where the stain still lingered underneath.

TWENTY-FIVE

I'm waiting for Ted to come home. Still nursing my bladder, still trying to make sense of my ever-crustier, flaky grey skin. I have never told Ted about my dreams or visions, especially not the baby-related ones. It would only affirm him in his world view. He has this tendency to reduce all my feelings to procreative yearning. His equivalent of "she's on her period". I buy furniture because I want children. What I really want is to fill my house with tiny feet, not elegant chair legs. I "nag" him because I have too much time on my hands, unlike his friends' wives who are appropriately distracted by their offspring. Everything I do, everything I want, is just a desperate cry for the children I can't admit to myself I want. Ted himself shows no interest in the screaming heads wrapped in blankets his friends bring to brunches, only directing my attention to them: "Why don't you have a cuddle?" he says and returns to his sausage and eggs. Babies are just pacifiers for women. With all Ted's talk of babies, it is no wonder they dominate my nightmares.

The seat was now so wet it was hard to tell if I'd removed the stain or not. I kept scrubbing for good measure. My phone was buzzing like a crazed critter from its spot on the rug. I assumed it was Mother wanting to reconcile, or manipulate me into visiting, or inviting herself over, given that she was now single and free and wild and so would happily adventure into the suburbs. Just the thought of it made me want to rip the fabric off the chaise longue. I left the phone ringing until the whole room seemed to be buzzing with its vibrations. Then I picked it up to cancel the call, only to see that it was Jenny, not Mum, chasing me like a determined Rottweiler. I cancelled it anyway. She was probably just calling to make excuses, to complain about her affair blowing up in her ugly, annoying face. Tina was right. Women nowadays were just full of excuses. Refused to take responsibility for the consequences of their choices. They were all spoiled, fickle, weak. Cancel.

I scrubbed harder at the stain. I was beginning to wear away the indigo blue of the cloth to white. Clean, that's all that mattered. Worn fabric was better than toxic grease. I scrubbed for another ten minutes. The phone rang again. I checked it. It was Jenny. I hung up. I repeated that cycle a few times, then decided I'd finished cleaning. I got up and looked down at the patch I'd cleared. It was good; naked, pure. Like skin.

I put the baking powder away. Then returned to the chair to sit down and recover. But that was impossible, because the stain was still there. Now that the round white patch had dried, I could see that it contained an iris of resilient grease, staring at me, refusing to let me rest. I returned to the kitchen, put on the rubber gloves. This time I decided on chemical warfare: bleach. I didn't trust myself with the entire bottle in the heat of the moment. I had to ration myself. I tilted the bottle to pour a little onto a cloth. *Gently does it*, I heard Wendy's voice say, *this stuff will scorch you*. I jolted at the thought of Wendy's interfering turkey neck bustling its way into my business. Mothers. Bloody mothers. Bleach squirted violently from the bottle; I turned my face away to shield my eyes. I turned back to assess the damage. Most of it had missed me, just a splatter on the tiled floor. I reached down to wipe it away and noticed a droplet had landed on my wrist. It was burning into me. I watched it fizzle on my skin, waiting for the pain to come. It had landed on the inside of my wrist, the whitest, veiny part that looked translucent like a baby's temples. I watched the bleach scorch that delicate part of me, watched the skin turn pink in the shape of a kidney bean, or an embryo. I thought, maybe this could be the baby Ted and I would never have.

I stood up with none of the urgency required to prevent a chemical burn. I wanted it to scar me. I wanted a souvenir from a time I knew I'd have to conjure up if I ever needed the strength to run. I patted at the spot half-heartedly, then picked up the cloth by my feet and returned to the chaise.

The phone rang again. It was Jenny. I hung up. I continued, scrubbed until the phone started again, incessant in the way only Jenny knew how to be. I scrubbed and hung up, repeated that cycle twenty, maybe thirty times.

Until Ted walked in. I hadn't heard his keys in the lock like I usually did. He'd become stealthier. I looked up, slightly embarrassed, from my spot on the floor, aware that I was sweating from scrubbing the spot he'd been sitting on.

"Trying to scrub away my essence?"

"Of course not, darling, just a little stain, that's all."

He nodded, not deeming the discussion worth having.

"Ted?" I said, without knowing what I wanted to ask him.

He stopped, sighed and turned. "Yes?" he said, sarcastic.

I racked my brains for something that wouldn't seem trivial to him.

"What do you want for dinner?" It was the best I could come up with.

"Don't mind. I'll be going out after."

"Pub?"

He shrugged, which I assumed either meant that it was true but he didn't think it mattered, or that he was actually going to see another woman and couldn't be bothered to lie. Either way, his distinct apathy cut into me and hollowed me out like a knife carving out a pumpkin.

"Perhaps I'll do a pumpkin stew," was all I could think to say.

He shrugged again and disappeared up the stairs. I looked at the stain; it was still there. Only I'd run out of steam. It seemed hopeless anyway. I dropped myself on the sofa. My phone rang again. It was Jenny. I hung up.

I wanted to give up. I wanted to order takeaway and watch romcoms and ignore Ted until, perhaps, he left me. So that it wouldn't be my fault. But then the thought of the agony of his disappearance and the shattered dreams he'd leave behind turned my stomach inside out. That, and the mortification of having to admit to my mother that my relationship, too, had failed. That reanimated me. Besides, the state of the universe was so volatile. I had to be careful.

I made pumpkin stew and took a picture of the bowl on the kitchen table beside a whole interestingly textured pumpkin; then of the bowl and the pumpkin and some scattered autumnal leaves I'd gathered from the garden; then of just the pumpkin and the leaves and a few homemade oat biscuits I had left over; then of the oat biscuits and the leaves and a perfectly arranged trail of crumbs on the rustic wooden tabletop; then of just the crumbs up close so that you could see the grain of the wood in the table – so rustic. Then I posted them as a series, with the hashtags #autumn #fall #autumnvibes #instaggood #halloween #herbst #naturelovers #autumnleaves #autumncolours #nature #naturephotography #leaves #art #photooftheday #housewife #homemaker #wife #love #housewives #housewifelife #women #home #feminine #lifestyle #cooking #cleaning #homedecor #aproncladarmy #house #beauty #foodporn #laundry #retro #desperatehousewives #housework #follow #goodhousewife #sexywife #femininity #femininewomen #femininesisters #femininefamily #femininity #femininewisdom #naturalfeminity #femininityispower #femininewomanhood #portrait #prettywoman #style #queen #instagood #bestlife.

Then I served Ted cold stew.

TWENTY-SIX

I'm waiting for Ted to come home. You start to notice new things about your body in the dead of night. Hear new sounds. Track new movements. Stomach grows fuller with bile. Poo moves like a slug through your bowels. Hairs on your arms, legs, face, neck, rise and fall with each suggestion of a breeze.

The sounds get louder with each beat of the night. Tree branches creak, wind swoops, perhaps the echo of ambulance sirens in the distance. Your body's sounds join the world's sounds, move out into the night and cascade through the hollow ether until you are living in that dark endlessness that is now also the abandoned inside of your body. And you feel so small in that boundless landscape; jittery and unanchored like a fugitive in the corporeal desert you'd once deluded yourself was your own.

It was five o'clock, and I was chopping the onions for an autumnal savoury tart when my phone rang. It was Ted. Telling me he wouldn't need dinner. Working late, he said. I hung up.

I wasn't sure if we were getting more honest or more ruthless. Our phone calls were easier now, our exchanges seamless, accepting. No longer made with bated breath, no longer with the nervousness of trying to make things right. It was like he accepted that I would be disappointed in him, always was. His voice was steady when he broke the bad news – home late, pub tonight, no time to accompany me on another trip to the showroom – like he was proud of himself, for the way he was standing up for himself, and for giving me no expectations.

The phone rang again. It was Jenny. This time I answered.

"To what do I owe this pleasure?"

"Someone could have died." I wondered if she'd forgotten – the last time someone had died, she'd shown me how little loss meant to her.

"What do you want, Jenny?"

"Your mum found out about me and Barney."

I moved my face closer to the onions, trying to procure tears, testing if anything could pierce through my newfound state of apathetic numbness. Was this the balance Tina was talking about?

"And what do you want me to do about it?"

"I just thought you'd want to hear it from me."

"What on earth made you think that?"

"I wasn't sure if you were speaking to your parents, so, I don't know. I just wanted to do the right thing."

"Could have thought of that before."

"So you are upset, about your dad and me." She sounded almost gleeful. "You seemed so calm about it the other day. I thought it made sense, in a way. Your parents' marriage was so far gone."

"I'm not upset. I'm exhausted. Mum's right about you. She always told me, but I wouldn't listen. You're completely uninteresting. Everyone thinks so. You're not fooling anyone with your yoga voodoo hogwash. Even if I did believe in that stuff, the way you talk about it is ridiculous. You're just a sour, fat bitch, and tight leggings and mantras aren't going to fix that."

I was pleased with my speech. It was concise, vicious, and hit all the key insecurities. It was definitely enough to get yet another irritating woman off my back.

"This is all about the curse, isn't it?" She was relentless.

"Your idiotic curse was just one in a chain of manipulative, egotistical pranks you pulled on me, Jenny."

"It must be difficult, living in this state of uncertainty."

"I don't believe in nonsense. Now will you leave me alone?"

"I did it for both of us, you know. I thought maybe we'd move up in the social ranks together, but then you ditched me."

It was official. She was actually deranged. Couldn't look beyond her relentless need to control me. She wouldn't stop until she she'd ruined my life. I was sure of it.

"Go to hell, Jenny." It seemed like an appropriate goodbye. I hit the big red button to end the call, then went on Instagram. I opened up her cringeworthy page, "the_yogi_next_door", and let my thumb hover over the screen before I did the unthinkable: I unfollowed her. She didn't deserve another moment of my attention. It would be me, not the devil, who refused her a story.

I banished her and then threw on an apron, grabbed a spatula, and went and stood in front of the silver-rimmed mirror in the hall. I raised my middle finger and snapped a shot of my reflection. I posted a picture of myself with the caption "& God still blessing me", then added the hashtag #bitchyoubreakfast for good measure. I was smug. It was perfectly on brand, ensuring that it would reach my followers, with a good dose of targeted malice that only Jenny would understand. Like hashtags, the most effective attack is a balance of poignancy and reach.

TWENTY-SEVEN

I'm waiting for Ted to come home. Three, four years, maybe more. I'm losing track of just how long I've been waiting. My body is now so stiff and cold I wonder, if, when I do ever decide to get up, I will even be able to drag my leaden limbs across the room. If Ted never returns, I'll die cold and alone, like I'd always feared, only all the more tragic because it will have happened in secret, under the guise of the happy life I'd always wanted. I allow myself a flex of the wrists. I stroke the patch on the seat under me: raw, worn, tender. More honest than the pristine seat I'd planned for us.

I've been getting it all wrong. All this time I've spent trying to become an influencer, when really the key is to be influenced. That is real love. And to be influenced is to give your soul away. I'd been afraid to let Ted take mine. I'd been pushing him away from the moment I barred crumbs from the bed, or red wine from the sofa; from the moment I'd chosen furniture over forever. I'd been trying to preserve the accents of me that punctuated our house, afraid that, if I didn't, I'd be reduced to an echo of Ted. And then, I'd gone even further. I'd been afraid of merging into Ted, but I'd engulfed him instead; had tried to ingest him, to make him part of my dream because I didn't really trust him, never really believed him, when he said he'd make me a part of his.

I close my eyes until the ballerina appears in front of me. I watch her turn her body, her delicate little fingers high above her head, the arch in her spine creating a wave in the gold and glass that rippled with the reflection of every twirl. I watch her for as long as I can, knowing that it is the last time.

With Ted gone, the stain seemed worth returning to. I spent the day googling various cleaning products, although the most accomplished housewives agreed that simple household items beat any brand of cleaner. I tried salt, corn starch, talcum powder. I tried dish soap, and then concoctions including all of the above. Then I'd set into the stain with abandon. Letting my hand circle and dig and rub and send me into a sweaty trance.

In between the rounds of annihilation, I took deep breaths and lit #yogic #candles to find my #Zen, which worked on the whole but occasionally reminded me of Jenny. I channelled those bursts of outrage into composing a masterful shot of the candles in the near-dark, with Jenny's much-loved quote "Don't let them dim your light", adding the hashtags #zenhome #zenspace #zenlife #fengshui and then #bitchyoucantkillmyvibe for good measure – karmic cleansing for the idiot who thought she could curse me.

Equilibrium, that's what my life was. I'd show Jenny the true meaning of Zen. Tina-style. Old school. Nothing said "fuck you, bitch" like a perfect relationship and a perfect house and pure euphoric happiness.

*

The day he asked me to move in. We were on our way home from the pub. He'd had a few, of course, which perhaps explained his animated mood. We'd been talking about it for a long time. The drive up to my family's estate was starting to grate and we never really got to be alone, he said. Spending nights at his was fun and all, but somehow the distance made him feel like we were always choosing between two imperfect options.

"We come from different worlds, but that doesn't matter. We can make a life that feels right for both of us." He was so naively adorable: his eyes wide with enthusiasm, as if he'd just landed on an epiphany. Totally unaware that his destiny had long been set in stone. "We're like Romeo and Juliet. That's what you girls like, isn't it?" His chauvinism was still cute in those days. Then, he gave me the speech.

"Rosie, babe." He took my hands in his. "Before we met, my life wasn't real." He shook his head, struggling to find the words. He hadn't had much practice. "It was jokes, you know, it was fun. I got to be Ted the businessman at work, Ted the lad with the... lads."

He stopped again, mumbled "stupid" under his breath, frustrated with his own inarticulacy, but he persevered. It was worth it. It was for us. "Ted the son on Sundays." He sighed. "It was like I was three people, but I wasn't anyone." He rolled his eyes at his triteness, but he pulled me in closer. "When I was sitting at the table tonight, I didn't get it, why suddenly none of it was laughs and banter like it used to be. I was on top form when I was getting ready, hair looking good, crisp shirt, you know: the works. But I was out of it, their voices all like jumbled, they weren't funny." He frowned, a sadness in his eyes I'd never seen before. The death of comedy was a serious matter. "Suddenly it hit me why. And it feels so good. I saw Barry's face, him looking at me like I was a snob because I didn't want another pint, and it made me happy because I knew I didn't want any of it anymore. What does Barry know about love? You know. I'll take us away, babe – somewhere we can be alone and build something real. Rosie, do you get me? Even if I could still find it in me to pretend to be mates with Barry and them, it would be a lie, like, like… a sin to pretend to love them like I love you." He looked pleased with himself now, like he'd broken through a lifetime's silence. He clenched my hands even tighter. "Let's move in together."

"It's a great plan," I'd told him, surprised and relieved that he could speak, even had a preference for some words over others, a will. And in that moment that didn't seem the problematic hindrance it later did, only made me like him more. "But are you sure you can leave it all behind? We'll be alone. And I'll be a foreigner in a new country. I'll depend on you for everything."

He liked that. He stroked my hair and held my chin. "I want you to depend on me, babe. I want to be your everything."

It was everything I'd wanted to hear. And I could tell it was everything he wanted to say. Equilibrium. Then he whipped out a brochure to the house of my dreams. "I came across this one at work and I thought of you." It was perfect. The house I'd described to him down to a tee. The man who listened. The attentive provider. This was what people warned you about. Told you was too good to be true. But he was speaking like he was in my head; like he'd been a fly on the wall of my childhood dreams. "Big talkers never deliver," Mum had always said, probably to reconcile herself with her own mute of a man, but Ted's actions made his words look small.

"You can do with it whatever you like. You said you wanted to do interior design, didn't you? Now you can." He proceeded to paint the perfect picture. He pointed out the corners on the floorplan where he'd build shelving, the alcove with all the sun, the front garden with the white picket fence, and the quaint little path leading to the door. He kissed me on my cheek between passages and passages about the life we would share, how he'd go to work and come home and I'd show him all the things I'd done, and then we'd eat together and talk and laugh like we did now, but every day, and then we'd make "passionate love", he called it, every single day. I'd never heard him so verbose, or so certain. And none of it seemed impossible; we wanted a simple life, just the important things, none of the drama or the politics or the money that misled people. Without all of that getting in the way, just the two of us, we both thought, we would finally have something real.

When the memory ended, when I awoke to the present reality of my life, in front of me appeared my hand scrubbing that same dirty patch on the chaise longue, and it looked suddenly older, brown spots and veins covering skin leatherier than I remembered. Somehow fifteen years had passed since Ted had offered me that pretty picture. I must have been cleaning unconsciously this entire time. Distracted, I suppose, by my dreams of the life I was trying to build. Staring at the old hand and the old sofa, I found myself wondering why Ted had to go and ruin everything with his ugly stain. The bleach scar was still there. I dropped the cloth and used my freed-up hand to stroke my little pink embryo with one finger, lovingly, soothing the sting as I pressed down against the sore, exposed skin.

Then when I lifted the finger, a pang, and the pain was back, not agonising but constant, and I realised that it was always there, each and every day.

A flutter in my gut, a wisp and a slither that made me think of giving up. Where was he? He said he'd be there for me, that he'd give up his friends and his life and always put me first. But now it looked like I was the only one who'd really sacrificed. The one left scrubbing by herself in this abandoned shell of a home. I panicked. I was losing it – the will. Something had to be done. I dropped my hands to the floor and pushed myself up to standing. I walked outside, down the narrow path, through the picket fence, then the ten steps that took me up and through to the identical door next to mine. I knocked on Tina's door, and I asked her what to do.

TWENTY-EIGHT

I had tried to swallow him whole. As a child, when Dad read me *Little Red Riding Hood*, that was my biggest fear: that a girl lost in the woods might be eaten whole, not in pieces. Now I know it's scarier to be eaten in pieces. To lose all sense of your anatomy, to forget where your foot should be or your shoulder, to forget how they fit together to make a body you used to feel at home in, and, perhaps, that used to feel things other than rejection and cold. Dad liked that fairy tale, maybe because it warned girls to stick to the straight and narrow, maybe because it justified his ideas about killing to survive.

Even scarier than being eaten in pieces, though, is eating someone else and finding yourself unable to digest them. The worst part is that it makes me feel fat. Not attractively voluptuous in that curvaceous Pre-Raphaelite way Ted used to say I was. I'm swollen in the middle, pregnant with death. It's all a pretty hopeless situation, given that the only movement that could resolve my debilitated state would be a movement of the bowels, or a stillbirth – the definition depends on how much value I decide to give to the life I've carried around with me all these years. It depends on whether or not I decide a relationship can have any value, without its happily ever after.

At school, they once let us read a shocking version of *Little Red Riding Hood*, one in which she saves herself. She tells the wolf, disguised as her grandmother, that she needs to defecate and wouldn't want to do so in bed. Surprisingly, unbelievably, the wolf lets her go, still tied by a string, mind. It seemed out of character for the cunning animal to give his victim leeway, but I always figured mention of her intestines had killed the mood. Maybe I'd been onto something, making myself ugly to Ted, buying myself space and time, while I figured out how to slip that flimsy cord that bound us. Perhaps I sensed that what I thought was a fairy tale was really a trap.

It would have been easier to shit the bed, of course. But I wasn't brave enough. I let myself be talked out of it. On the verge of escape, I returned to the wolf, knowing now that he no longer desired me. I stayed because I couldn't imagine myself in a different story. I tightened the string. I tried to fix the mess I'd made. And I blamed him for not loving the woman who had tried to escape him. I blamed him for my own betrayal. I blamed him for my own cowardice. I was ashamed of myself. I deserved to be naked. I deserved to be ugly and on display and he deserved to look at me and tell me what an ugly beast I was.

I'm not afraid anymore. I'm cold and alone, but I'm finally facing the consequences of a life on the run. I am where I want to be. My body is calm. The cramps in my muscles, the movement of my bowels, the itching where my skin touches the velvet, all of it has settled. I've finally transcended my own self-indulgent bodily needs. At five in the morning, I hear the keys in the lock.

A foot on the mat, the tapping of a suit shoe on the hard, wooden floor. One, then two points of patent leather appear on the rug in front of me. I look up at Ted's shadow of a face above.

"What the hell are you doing?"

Smoke and cheap lager waft down towards me, displacing sweet lavender with the remnants of his night.

He doesn't like it. I knew he wouldn't. He is even, possibly, slightly disgusted. I know I deserve it, but I can't take it. I sink back down into my flesh. I want to sit up, to turn away. A single bat of those disinterested eyelids is all it takes. I want to protect myself from his spiteful gaze, to wrap my arms around myself to cover my shame and hide. I am weak, soft and human. I've been over-zealous; this punishment is too much for anyone to bear.

The problematic and frightening reality of the situation is, however, that as much as I want to flee the situation I've created, I find myself entirely unable to move. My arms lie paralysed by my side, my legs crooked and stiff from their hours of inactivity; my face, already cracked before, is now ossified. I am a human relic.

Ted looks down at me, waiting for me speak. I think, I hope, he might shake me, that perhaps that will return blood and life to my limbs. But he does nothing. After an unbearable pause, he finally grunts, clears his throat, and turns away.

He leaves me here – all night, then the following day, and all the days after that. He never acknowledges me again. As far as he is concerned, I've become one with the chair that to him had always seemed equally useless.

The house gathers dust, and so do I. Without me there to do the cleaning, my pristine shrine, my life's work, degenerates into chaos and filth. And because I can't move, there is nothing to do but to let it happen, to let myself fade under the room's shroud.

Only my eyes are active. They scan the room in circular motions like the hand of the clock, looking for purpose. Sometimes they rest on the scar on my wrist. I still love that scar, how it adorns my body like jewellery. Better than anything Ted ever bought me. Better than the ring that meant nothing. Most of the time, though, my eyes are on him. They see how he eats his microwave dinners on the sofa. They watch along with him the entirety of *Game of Thrones*. They observe, and I can do nothing when he rubs grease and crumbs into the furniture. I lie there, and I let it all happen. I take it all in.

I see, and I hear. I hear Tina ring the doorbell a week or two after I first turned to stone. Hear Ted shout without moving from the sofa for her to "go away". Then, when she persists that she'd like to know where I am, hear him, now slumped half on sofa, half on the ground, tell her that I am "indisposed… forever". I listen how Tina tells him ever so politely that if he doesn't let her in, she'll have to force an entry. I listen as he takes a swig of beer.

I hear Tina return an hour later with a spanner and wrench the door open. I feel myself momentarily comforted by the confident swish of garments that moves through the doorway and into the hall.

TWENTY-NINE

When Tina enters the room, she finds lying on the sofa a splendid portrait of Rosie as she had last seen her, in all the wonder of her exquisite youth and beauty.

Lying on the floor is a man, in jogging bottoms, beer in his left hand, remote control in his right. He is sunken, crumpled, belching, with a bloated red face.

"You must be Ted. She always spoke of you so fondly."

Ted looks up at Tina, dazed and weary, deep, dark circles under his vacant eyes.

"Let's have a look at her." Tina makes her way to the side of the battered old chaise longue, the shape of which she recognises from the day she'd watched the men unload it from the back of a van. The day she had tried to warn me of the repercussions of such a frivolous acquisition.

"Recalcitrance. I always said it would be the death of her."

Tina leans in closer, her neckline gaping, exposing her breasts. I want her even closer. I want her arms around me, cradling me until warmth returns to my veins.

"It is a cosmic tragedy," she mumbles.

Ted vaguely lifts an eyebrow but doesn't move.

"These stubborn girls." She strokes the side of my face. I'd always imagined her thin hands would be cold, but they glow, like the dark green heat of lizard skin in the desert sun. Her emerald eyes sink into me.

"Oh, but I mustn't be ungenerous. She did try. It's my fault really. My timing isn't what it used to be. I should have recognised that she was too far gone. She just couldn't find the levity required for flight. Stuck, she was stuck in her own seriousness."

Tina stands up. My heavy soul cries out as it tries to pull her back. But she's right, it is too heavy, and it is too late. I watch Tina take a good look at Ted.

"I always imagined she was being melodramatic when she described you as a lumbering oaf." She turns back and strokes my face once more. "Curious."

Tina raises her other hand, which I hadn't noticed, given my narrow field of vision, holds a rolled-up newspaper. She unrolls the crusty pages. I inhale the smell of ink on cellulose, from a time before people had written themselves out of their roots. Tina leans over, one final time, and props the paper up against the arm of the chaise, facing me. She knows that my sight is all I have left. She knows that I'm still doomed to watch my tragedy unfold.

"A crisis of ossification," she announces, then turns to leave.

Don't leave me. I conjure the forces Tina had made me believe existed. I roll my eyeballs towards Ted. This is the moment for telepathy. This is the moment for selfless magic. I need Ted to tell her. That I'd tried. That my friendship with Tina had meant something, everything. He didn't hear me, of course – we aren't connected in that way. Maybe if I'd done my duty, things would have been different. Instead, he utters to her the rather less empathic words, "Don't be too hard on yourself. She's always been off her rocker."

THIRTY

I listen to the opening theme of *Game of Thrones*, its epic drama drawing attention to my own immobility. No more adventures for me. Then I turn to the article Tina had left me.

They call it an epidemic. Women all over the country locked into their bodies. Some frozen like me, others stuck in what the paper called neurotic spasms, taking pictures of themselves for all eternity. One girl's shoulder dislocated. They dragged her into hospital, her arm still extended, clicking selfies. One girl is eerily reminiscent of Jenny. A marathon yoga photoshoot left her tied up in a figure of eight, limbs glued together by molten spandex. There is a picture of the yogi Instagrammer, but her face is indiscernible. It is unmissable though, how the folded-up body perfectly resembles an infinity symbol; Jenny would have liked that, being the symbol of a generation. Her pact with the devil finally realised.

Besides Tina, no one visits. Not Wendy, not my own mother, not Jenny or Dad. When it really comes down to it, no one is keeping track of my existence. As I lie in quiet solitude, I try to figure out if I'm now part of Tina's collection or Ted's. Do I belong in Tina's cabinet of curiosities or Ted's history of broken hearts? A museum of tragic romance either way. Tina would agree, at least, that I got to write my own story.

Time passes and Ted degenerates in front of me while I stay exactly the same – every part of me fixed in time. Everything, apart from my bush, which mocks me, growing wilder and wilder, reminding me of a time when I had a choice. It spreads like vines down the side of the chaise longue and across the floor, tickling Ted's feet, triggering the twitch of a toe on one of our more dynamic days.

At first, I think that I've pushed everyone away, that they've given up on me, that this explains the total lack of visitors. In a more optimistic moment it occurs to me – early morning, while Ted is still asleep – that maybe people take me seriously at last, finally believe what I've been telling them all these years: that I'm happy, that I've found what I've been looking for. That Ted and I really are meant to be.